THE NURSERY

THE NURSERY

Szilvia Molnar

Pantheon Books
New York

Grateful acknowledgment is made for permission to reprint previously published material:
An excerpt from "Summons," from *Human Hours,* by Catherine Barnett. Copyright © 2018 by Catherine Barnett. Reprinted with the permission of The Permissions Company, LLC, on behalf of Graywolf Press, Minneapolis, Minnesota, graywolfpress.org. An excerpt from *Float* by Anne Carson. Compilation copyright © 2016 by Anne Carson. Used by permission of Alfred A. Knopf, an imprint of the Knopf Doubleday Publishing Group, a division of Penguin Random House LLC. All rights reserved.

Library of Congress Cataloging-in-Publication Data
Name: Molnar, Szilvia, author.
Title: The nursery : a novel / Szilvia Molnar.
Description: First edition. New York : Pantheon Books, 2023.
Identifiers: LCCN 2022037320 (print). LCCN 2022037321 (ebook).
ISBN 9780593316849 (hardcover). ISBN 9780593316856 (ebook).
Subjects: LCSH: Postpartum depression—Fiction. Motherhood—Fiction. LCGFT: Psychological fiction. Novels.
Classification: LCC PS3613.O476 N87 2023 (print) | LCC PS3613.O476 (ebook) | DDC 813/.6—dc23/eng/20220809
LC record available at https://lccn.loc.gov/2022037320
LC ebook record available at https://lccn.loc.gov/2022037321

www.pantheonbooks.com

Jacket design by Linda Huang

Printed in the United States of America

First Edition
2 4 6 8 9 7 5 3 1

For Ryan

... from within the walls
of my exhausted mothermind.

—Catherine Barnett, "Summons"

... what exactly is the relation of madness to translation?
Where does translation happen in the mind?

—Anne Carson, *Float*

THE NURSERY

As hard as it can, the August sun pushes itself into our small apartment on the third floor. The baby I hold in my arms is a leech, let's call her Button. Button is crying. She recently entered the world, violently and directly. We are alone and cocooned in our two-bedroom apartment until we are not, because there's a knock on the door. The foreign sound makes Button cry harder and makes me unsure of what to do. I have been a mother for as long as Button has been outside of me, and I have yet to embrace the title as much as I have had to embrace her.

Here, the air is motionless, the light is direct, and sounds echo off the walls. I'm sweating.

I place Button in a cushioned container by the couch in the living room and she makes disappointed sounds, large and unkind. I make a different decision. I pick her up and move my robe to the side as I bring her body across my chest. It's a motion that I still fumble through, her weight is alien to what my mind expects to hold and my own body heats up another notch. Smells on us and around us bring attention to themselves, I am brought to discomfort and cringe at my current state. The day has been long and lonely.

One arm and a hand control the body of the baby, the other

unclicks the nursing bra to get the breast out. My nipple shines dark brown in the late afternoon light and I am reminded that the golden hour is my favorite hour to walk around in the city where we reside.

Before Button arrived, I walked everywhere and leaving the apartment was a simple undertaking. During a break from the library or my writing desk where most of my work takes place, I often ventured out onto the busy streets and hoped that the beat of the city would kick a word or two out in front of me, some phrase, idea, or feeling that could be of use for whatever text I was translating at the time.

After almost ten years as a translator, my work was still mostly a struggle. Not necessarily the work itself, because there was pleasure in trying to get it "right" (a faulty concept that is still thrown around among fellow colleagues). Chameleoning my way forward was enjoyable, but the continuous fight for more money, grants, or God-forbid a royalty check was tiring. I wasn't the kind of translator to care but needed money as much as the next. Being in the periphery of the industry was also fine—the peculiar competitiveness mostly amused me. By now I knew a handful of editors who found me reliable and writers who liked my way of working. My recent translations were even getting accolades in the general press, which meant my name also occasionally appeared on book covers. Sometimes I would find the authors profiled in glossy magazines wearing thick wool sweaters, posing with brooding looks directed into the rugged Scandinavian landscape. Like any other ordinary person, I am too vain to deny that I didn't want to be photographed in the same cool milieu, but ultimately, I'm not the competitive kind. Visibility is not my desire.

I wasn't yet an orphan, but I had been moving away from family for so long that at some point I was walking away from the past, perhaps only to find myself content in the present. In literal terms, this meant making a modest life for myself in the States as a translator of Swedish literature.

As the sun is setting, I must leave these thoughts behind; I am here with Button and this is all I am. This is the doing, me being here.

With a hand on the back of her head, I put her face toward my nipple and a toothless mouth opens. She latches on with lips soft as a fish. I squirm from the initial discomfort of her bite.

Most of the time I don't know what I am doing. Button gets pushed so close to the breast that she may have a hard time breathing. Frustration arrives in her small bundle of a body and she screams, but her squeal is not loud enough to overpower the second round of knocking on the door. She makes me nervous. I wrangle with my arms. Again, there's knocking, harder. Again, I don't know what to do.

In a different state and in a different world I would have ignored the interruption and moved on with my life, and if I was expecting someone, I would have been prepared. Perhaps I can pretend that I'm getting ready for bed, make the robe appropriate and retie my hair. Perhaps I can blame my disheveled appearance on Button. Perhaps I can decide to never deal with the outside world again and perhaps whoever is behind the door can relieve me of this discomfort. Perhaps, in this battle, the choice has already been made for me.

I maneuver us toward the entrance and Button finally sucks rhythmically in between breaths. Her repetitive movements remind me of breaststrokes under water. As she slowly fills on the comfort brought from the milk, her body turns tranquil and gives in to satisfaction. I take a deep breath.

Through the peephole, I recognize the man as Peter, known to me as our upstairs neighbor. From the fish-eye lens, Peter's mostly bald head is enlarged like a balloon, and it is strung tightly to his long, slim body with a pair of beady eyes moving around, waiting for a reaction. I pause, unsure of what he would want at this hour. My husband, John, should be coming home any minute now anyway.

On each side of the door, the air is still. I open the door, wondering if maybe I asked for this.

After they put her on my chest in the early morning, I was like what you see scattered along a highway, an item once of value. I was a can of soda, a sock, a half-smoked cigarette, a piece of gum, a headless toy, or a pair of used underwear. I was the lonesome cap without its bottle. I had been run over and pushed to the side through traffic, wind, and other forms of aggression. At the same time, a dissipating high told me that I could do it all over again. It was the body tricking me into thinking that giving birth made me invincible.

In the rushed moments after Button was born, the room buzzed with nurses and doctors coming in and out, checking on me, checking on the baby, checking on information listed on screens, lines, and numbers here and there. Controls were pushed. Bedsheets, pillows, and crinkly paper covers were adjusted or discarded and replaced with fresh ones. Liquids poured out of me, liquids were pushed into my veins, and a catheter was pricked into my urethra.

The day was on wheels, including us, and next thing I knew we were being carted around. This is just one example of how life is made, and in my case it was done brutally. But I'm not sure it's possible to avoid brutality in birth. *Brut, brutus, bruto . . .* a man-made "beast" is not quite what I mean when wanting to describe the experience and yet it's the first thing that comes to mind.

Words and expressions flickered in front of my eyes, John bounced gently to and from, always in the way of someone trying to get to me and unsure of how to manage his presence around others. He said he was relieved that Button was born on the weekend, it helped him avoid taking time off from work, whereas I had no understanding of time, I only wanted to know where we were being taken.

While I was rolled down long, nondescript hallways, I kept thinking, *I give in to this moment.* I didn't have a choice.

In the evening, when the stream of hospital employees or our friends and John's family died down and the room was still as if I were forgotten, all I felt were my early exposed nipples sore from Button's first sucks. There were faint echoes of babies crying and nurses chatting in the background, indicating that the night shift would soon begin.

The lower part of my body was numb from medication, and with my crotch awkwardly wet from an ice pack melting between my legs, I wanted to twist her head.

Button had been with me for a handful of hours, she had been silent for most of this time, and there came an urge, as direct as hunger.

Let's wring you like a wet cloth.

The dark hospital room took my want and immediately threw it back at me.

It's a polite autumn day with people still eager to be outside before the winter will keep us in. I'm walking to meet John at our local Italian place where the East European waiters are indifferent to our presence but the food is cheap and cheerful. I can't help but think I will miss spending time alone with my husband. We are trying to get pregnant and it reminds me of our first months dating. Back then, we were often in a perpetual state of undress to dress and undress again, always helping each other wipe juices off of mouths and backs and stomachs, giggling while plucking tissues from their box, feeling younger than usual and forgetting what time it was. Now, newly married, I lie very still so as not to let any liquids drip out of me. My prenatal vitamins are taken regularly, and my ovaries are optimistic about the future.

In the meantime, our simple weekly routines continue. All while you are still a thought and I think about how I am going to resent you once you arrive. You will disrupt the peace. You will get in the way of my freedom. It's possible you may one day ask for an apology, I'm just being honest. I want you as much as I fear you.

I stroll up to the neon-signed restaurant and spot John through the window. Such a pretty man, made more handsome from a distance. A waiter nods me over to a booth where John is sitting reading on his phone. Because he is in love with me, John notices when I enter the restaurant and puts his phone away. He watches as I come closer and I quickly swoop in next to him because he likes it when we see the same things, a detail he once shared with me. We kiss. We give quick recaps of our days: his at the office, mine at the library.

John plays with the salt and pepper shakers on the table. He must be hungry. We make little half-moon piles of salt next to our fresh glasses of water and ignore the grimace from the waiter as he takes our order. We lean on each other in the booth and don't say much until the food arrives.

Once John gets to tear into a roughly sliced white baguette, dipping uneven pieces in olive oil, with one arm around me, he becomes animated. Tells me about an article he recently read on how advantageous it is for people in northern Africa to educate themselves on climate change because it allows them to better prepare and maintain their farms or crops.

I dip the crusty bread in mediocre olive oil and chime in or ask questions where I can. When I am with John, I am always myself. Sitting and listening to him makes me wonder if the word "compatible" is in any way connected to "compassion."

A Greek salad is placed in front of us, as well as a generous bowl of spaghetti pasta with sausage and broccoli rabe. We divide the food diplomatically and trade plates with our movements synced, easy. The restaurant buzzes with other people's friends and family occupying most tables. The room feels alive, happy, and hungry. The waiters rush in and out of the kitchen to get filled plates through the door, crisscrossing their way around each other. I describe a new translation that I'm working on to John, about a woman who has lost her husband to suicide only days after their son is born, and her recap of them meeting and dating and then getting married makes you think, as the reader, that she drove her partner to killing himself. It's a terribly long book, *too long.*

But there's nothing stylistically challenging about it, so it'll be a quick one.

I twist the pasta around my fork and collect pieces of rabe.

I should be done by Christmas, and the money is good this time around.

We talk about what we would do with the money; maybe save some, maybe travel with some, although John can rarely get away from work.

With a body that has relaxed into fullness from the food, he starts mocking me.

What is it with Scandinavians and their obsession with death?

What do you mean? I know exactly what he means.

Someone always dies in your books. He cleans the remaining traces of food and oil on his plate with a last piece of bread.

That can't be true. I give him a grin. *Also, they're not "my" books.*

Sure they are he says, and reminds me that the last four books I translated were about a wife getting cancer, a son overdosing, then a child dying, and then a mother dying right after giving birth.

Okay, I admit that that's a fair amount of death.

At least it pays for rent I add casually.

True. Maybe your own book could be about the opposite he says good-humoredly, and I tell him to stop being silly but appreciate how he thinks about me. We ease into the end of the year with little resistance.

I don't remember waking up because I don't remember falling asleep. It's light outside and I am resting in bed. I'm still an item thrown away, similar to those first two days at the hospital with Button. I'm reliving the birth all over again, aren't I? I am stuck in a déjà vu.

I hear John in the other room, so he can't answer my question, and Button certainly can't help. Pieces of eye crust stain my pillow. An innocent down feather that somehow found itself on the sheet at the edge of the bed sways once in the still room. The light shining through the window makes it twinkle in a subdued way. The bassinet next to me is empty, which allows my mind to entertain the thought that Button is forever gone and I can go back to my desk like before. I picture sitting all alone with elbows resting on the wooden table and the pen sketching the first draft of a translation or jotting down scenarios of my own. Serene in the waters of interpretation and pleased with my own company, I sink deeper and deeper into a story that is held up by love, jealousy, despair, tragedy, death, and inheritance.

The midday light and my weighted body suggest that a few days have passed since giving birth and I remain exhausted from beyond my core. This would probably be viewed as pretty bad writing if it were published, but it is the simple truth. My core. John often mocks me for eating everything but the calyx of an apple or the stem of a pear.

Still lying in bed, I hear a faint murmur of visitors, his friends and family saying

The first weeks are so hard.

There's hard and there's hard.

There are cement walls that are hard to break through and there's a hard cock. There's a hard night's sleep and there's a body that has hardly had more than two hours of consecutive rest and for how long? This is what "hard" does to the mind and that hard body is my body and my body is so tired it is losing me, walking away. My shadow lying underneath me is so slow you could catch it by the tail if I set off running, and there is no way I can set off.

In bed, my belly is staring back at me, bloated and neglected. *Is this my core? Is this the core of me?*

I poke and push the excess flesh around. My fingers sink deep, disappearing in funny bulges of stretched skin. It doesn't hurt; it is her absence protruding, moving awkwardly around like a water bed. My breasts tingle. A blood-filled pad between my legs needs changing. I can sense its weight against one thigh. I hope I haven't stained the bed. It wouldn't be the first time in this short amount of time.

I hear louder noises from the other room and now the full, sober realization of Button not being attached to me makes me leap out of bed. I'm having a heart attack. I get down on the ground and roll around because I am covered in flames. My actions are not springlike, there are still places that I didn't know could ache. But, yes, I am on fire if she is not with me. A slow flow of milk leaks out into my bra, staining it in big blotches. The metamorphosis from giving birth has left me unrecognizable to myself. I stand up and try to cover this new self, wrapping layers of clothing around my unshapely body. Some bone in me creaks, as harshly as an old wooden floor. Random and weird pains from my stomach emerge, then dissipate. I must hide this character, I must hide myself from John.

Why is your coffee cup in the freezer? John asks with his head in the cold compartment. He is cradling Button with one arm like a quarterback protecting a football, and I stand behind them in the open kitchen, awkwardly empty-handed, not knowing what to say. Feeling the strap of the robe around my waist; knowing I could sleep for days. The cool air from the fridge escapes and disappears into the living room.

Give her to me I say.

I don't know what you're talking about I say.

After some time, John comes to give hugs and kisses, and the soreness in my body reappears when he touches me.

You missed everyone. They all say hi. They're all so happy for us. He wants to keep touching me.

Please stop.

I sit down with Button on the couch and try to get comfortable by arranging and rearranging my hold around her.

What? I'm just saying…

John returns to the kitchen to ready a meal for us. He mumbles about how frustrated he is that he has to go back to work tomorrow, it's *too soon* after her birth. It is too soon, this can't be true, but it is and we knew this was coming. I will need to navigate this unexplored terrain from the apartment all by myself.

John places a plate of leftovers in the microwave and shuts its door. I start pulling my clothes aside for Button, trying not to panic.

When you don't sleep, you drop things. You put things in places where those things shouldn't be because they probably don't fit or belong there in the first place. Things appear only to disappear, and their purpose can't be utilized in the new place you've put them.

When you don't sleep you bump into your own doorframe, hit the edge of the countertop, bang your foot on every sharp corner. *That explains all of the bruises* your husband says, hinting at your clumsiness displayed on the corners of your body.

Things appear. Peter in the golden hour. You blink with one eye at a time and things disappear, similar to your words— the crutches to your "livelihood." The shape of the day turns unruly and unjust. The night is coming for you and you will have to meet it alone.

I turn to John with Button still in my arms.

Can you hear that?

The microwave dings.

Hear what? He takes the plate out of the microwave.

It's coming from upstairs I try to explain. *Some kind of wailing instrument.*

Unsatisfied with the temperature, John puts the plate back in. We both take a moment to listen, but all he hears is the boring droning sound of the microwave.

We need to get you more sleep he suggests so casually it should be an item I can pick up from a shelf in a store. The *We* in this situation sounds like a word taken from another language, not one that I can speak. What an easy thing for John to say, and the microwave dings a second time.

Your baby is crying Peter tells me before I've even opened the door fully. As if I can't hear the pitch of shrieking baby while she is secured in the nook of my arm. I can't believe I opened the door thinking that it would bring me some kind of comfort; instead I'm faced with having to explain myself to a random neighbor standing in front of me. Peter is a tall and meager-looking man with features that are reaching the end of aging. He leans slightly more on one leg, while Button stirs the air in the entryway. There's an oxygen tank right by his side with tubes slithering up and around him like vines on a tree. The man and the tank make an odd pair but clearly belong to each other.

I need sleep Peter says, directing his eyes on me. The consecutive knocks still echo faintly in my mind, right through and past my short hallway. He grips the tank so firmly he is holding on to time. I explain that there's nothing I would like more than to silence the baby.

The baby is upset he continues, and I can't tell if the man is perhaps autistic, senile, or simply annoying. Because I have no experience with autistic or senile people, I decide that he is annoying. He doesn't pick up on my wryness.

Button's cry is now a sloppy one, the kind without rhyme or reason, and I don't know how long I can hold this up. Her wails are bouncing off the walls and the walls of the apartment have broken off from top to bottom, they are ever so slowly closing in. This has to stop.

I take out a naked milk-filled breast and expect the man to turn away or pretend to turn away since I'm uncomfortable, insecure, and still fumbling my way through this action, but it's a necessary one and it's happening. There's a wheeze from Peter's oxygen tank, followed by silence. Oddly enough, it's the silence that unites us. Since we are witnessing a piece of nudity we are now all in this together. Stillness must be reached, and Button connects to the one thing that exists for her, and, finally, with a mouth full of breast, she starts to guzzle and quiets down. I cool off for a second.

I turn around and with blundering steps I bring Button to the living room. In this new silence, I hear how Peter's heavy cylinder makes a light *gadunk* when it hits the wooden floor of the apartment, and the door closes behind them. I am too spent to worry about who I have let in. The walls stand where they are for the moment. The sun's digression has put a hushed shade on the room.

You are not American my neighbor says, and it's easy to tell from that statement that Peter isn't either. We locate one another on a fictive map, compare the years and the recent places we have lived in the States. He is one of the oldest residents in the building and I feel young when he shares what the neighborhood looked like long before I moved in with John. Peter also appears in the apartment as half a person, someone clinging on to any form of company, since only discontent people knock on strangers' doors.

Does she hear music? he asks with a slight tilt of his chin toward Button, who is oblivious to everything else outside of what the breast provides. I admit that I haven't played her any music given that she is only a couple of days old. I close my arms around her tighter.

I played for my wife he continues, and I finally understand the source of the accent, how hard it is around the edges, always stressing the first syllable of each word, but mostly masked under decades of living away from his native country.

Not anymore. Peter taps the tank.

We are three empty columns. In this unity, I hear myself sharing details of my new life that I haven't shared with anyone.

Like the way the afternoon sun shades the apartment during these last weeks of the summer and the many shadows created at night. The depth, width, length of darkness will come up several times, and during these moments Peter will hold his tank firmly and portray his wife in exchange. He will talk about her in a way that insinuates that she is no longer around. Her death was so recent that he notices how her smell tries to linger in her clothes but keeps failing.

When he is too tired, Peter will say *I should sleep.* He will change his disposition and turn around in the living room, pulling his tank behind him. He will leave the door open but also an uneven trail of broken, dried leaves that used to be wedged in the wheels of the tank.

Sometimes, in order for Peter to return, I will take my pinky and unhook Button's lips that are tightly gripped around the nipple and I will let it sting, let the milk drip, only to let her resurrect her holler. Button will flail with her arms, pull out the red in her face, but it's worth it. Only to not be alone.

Our building houses a wide assortment of people. We are old and we are young, we come from far away or we have been here all along. When dinner is being made, pots are stirred and the stairway fills with the heated smell of spices. Whether we like · it or not, the scent of home, however differently interpreted by each of us, oozes from one place to another.

Packages arrive at the double-doored main entrance and if they are for a neighbor whose door you pass on the way to yours, you pick up the box and leave it outside of theirs. These small gestures hold the building up.

It's late in the morning, I hear how the first stream of neighbors has left the building, people are making their way to their daily jobs. I fill a mug with newly brewed coffee, slip my feet into a pair of shoes, and take it down with me to our stoop outside. The beverage is hot, black, and tastes of adulthood. Sipping a cup of coffee outside our building is a comforting habit. The morning air clears the head, the traffic of cars and people excites the mind, and the caffeine spikes the desire to work. I can't conjure a simpler way of starting the day before sitting down in front of my desk.

After a few weeks, the motions and patterns of neighbors become easily recognizable; most are of the predictable kind, too many carry a worried expression on their faces, and my mind turns to the dilemmas I have about my own work.

As much as I appreciate it, I can find moments when I get bored by the discourse around translation.

Grammar is useful but rules seem ridiculous. I mean, I abide by most rules and lean on fairness for my paid work, but I have also caught myself slicing out a sentence or two to make the translation, if not the original work, "better." Adaptation is my partner. Negotiations are necessary. And I am not shackled to the notion of accuracy, sometimes it's more important to indicate the direction of the motion presented by a word than to land on the correct one. The more I can connect with the author's intentions, the better I am at knowing what to reveal in my interpretation of their text. Honestly, I am more of an interpreter than anything else, but academics like to put significance on the capability of language. I suppose they are also right sometimes.

I suppose the answer is that there is no one answer.

It's hard for me to say how long I sit on the stoop with my coffee. I can see time in front of me, in the shape of the men and women making their way to places, some with children dragging their feet with too-heavy backpacks and then disappearing to be replaced by calmness, but I can't sense time within me. As wise as any respected guru, all I am is the sitting and all I am is the drinking of the coffee. I wouldn't be exaggerating if I said this is the happiest moment of my day. *The artist at work* is how John endearingly describes it when I tell him of my mornings on the stoop. He wants me to devote more time to my own writing, but I might be too unambitious to take him seriously. Still, John is not pushy and I suppose it's love when the person you are with doesn't expect anything from you in terms of productivity or performance. Such are the modest things one has the chance to ponder when you are not beholden to too many or too much.

The scent of dark-roasted beans clouds my face each time I take a sip and leaves my skin a little chilled in between tastes. Feeling the slight changes of the temperature, depending on the sun and the wind and the heat from the coffee, is a conversation worth having. At the same time, I watch the shadows across the street take form at the foot of the buildings.

Once my cup is empty, the flow of people has subsided and the morning turns into day. I return to the building and retreat to my desk. Nothing more, nothing less, but this is enough.

It starts in the early evening. The chills come at the same time as the fever, and they both make me want to leave my body. It's not that I want to first say my goodbyes around the room, taking my time, and then head on. I want to leave in a way where I'm climbing over people to get the hell out. This feverish state continues for about six hours. I know this because aside from the pain, there is nothing else that can pierce through my mind except for the passing of time. Somewhere in between these hours, I attach Button to the breast and with each suck she is ripping the skin off me. I'm exaggerating, but it's because I am right at the edge.

After hours of this madness, a searing pain shoots through each breast and it dawns on me that it is my milk coming in. That is what's driving me to climb the walls. So I go into survival mode, and as soon as I can I put Button down for a minute, I grab any ice packs that I can find from the freezer, and cover my chest like an exhausted sportsman. The ice is healing but also maddening. I don't understand what is happening under my chest.

I sit in this way until the ice packs are hot to the touch. When I need to nurse Button again, I am so uncomfortable that I almost throw up. My mind is trying to crawl out.

When I'm able to I put her aside, I move Button away from me like an item, turn on the hot water, and step in the shower after undressing. I turn around and let the sprays hit me between my shoulder blades, give the water all my gratitude. I try my best to stand upright. It scares me that I find myself shaking and I cover my face with my hands, not that John would be able to see me cry here anyway, but covering my face is the only thing I can do, otherwise I may do something unacceptable.

Galenskap! I think of the word "lunacy" then "moon" then how I don't even have the strength to howl.

Once I get out of the shower and have dressed again, I put Button on my chest regardless of what she wants in this moment because I need her to play her role in this. It's time to open the milk bar.

She better give me some relief.

The day we brought Button home from the hospital was characteristically hot and humid for the city. As if we brought back something alive in a box poked with holes, there was a newness in our space, a thing already murmuring in ways we couldn't understand. Our few belongings, our furniture, our carpets, bowls and shoes, my books and stacks and papers and the laptop, had all remained the same since her birth. My desk still stood firmly in a corner. So I walked around with the illusion that we—John and I—were also the same as before. Except I could barely walk. I definitely couldn't sit down. I wanted to lie down. It was all I wanted to do. It was all.

What was this? I asked myself.

Some kind of car crash and I could still feel the reverberations in the body. It had been dragged around like butchered meat soon to be stitched or stapled together. My clothes were suddenly too loose on my flattened shape and yet I was full, containing nothing but water. Milk and water. There may have still been some blood pumping to the heart.

Now the body needed to use the bathroom. At any given moment, it was a necessity. Funny how quickly I had lost the idea of "any given moment." *Momentum* implying something similar to "movement, motion, moving power" but also "alteration, change" over a "short time," having a longer duration than "an instant," *ett ögonblick,* a blink of an eye. As a puff of smoke giving in to air, I watched the moment disappear from me.

The sun imposed gravely into our small space, there was nowhere to hide, and I hoped to find a little peace in the bathroom. John was particular about wanting to play jazz upon Button settling into her new home. With his thumb he stroked his phone to find the right playlist, all while she squirmed unpredictably in my arms, resembling shellfish still alive on a chef's cutting board. To free up my hands, I placed her on the bathroom rug by the bathtub and started my attempt at peeing.

Afterward on the toilet, with disposable mesh underwear tangled around my ankles, I used a muscle relaxant taken from the hospital to numb some of the pain. When the spray hit the lips between my legs, a soothing feeling released and moved down to my thighs. I sensed it all the way up to my throat. I was curious about what I was actually spraying on my vulva and lifted the canister. The front of the tin alerted me to the fact that the spray was "For Athletes." I removed the soaked pad that was thick as a brick, rolled it up, and, in a meager throw, tossed it in a small bin that was next to the bathtub. Strange how quickly blood stops being frightening after giving birth. There was a large bag of pads under the sink, and from the toilet I maneuvered my arm to open the cabinet door to get a new one out. I stripped the back protective liner, scrunched that up to discard, and placed the new pad on the same mesh panty. I opened the jar-like container of thin witch-hazel pads and aligned them on the clean pad, one by one, as if I were assembling a deli sandwich. The disposable panty was already coming undone around the leg holes, with long threads hanging. I pulled the padded underwear up to my vulva and felt the stabbing of stitches.

The rest of the afternoon is spent on the couch getting used to the weight of Button in my arms and monitoring her first wet diaper, her first soiled diaper, first expulsion of air, first nap, the length, the weight, the color, the shape. Documenting, listing, noting, sometimes nodding off. Tracking and making sure she is alive while she is living. John enjoys the music he has picked. John texts pictures of Button to his family and friends. John leaves to run errands for us. Alone in the apartment, I assemble the pump as meticulously as an assassin with their cherished weapon. But I'm not as skilled with my gear yet and forget to attach the membranes or to use a cloth on my lap in case of drips. Spilling my own yellow drops of milk at this early stage appears strange and quickly turns invaluable. I start storing flimsy milk-filled bags in the freezer. What if the amount won't measure up to her hunger? The process of pumping does not excite me, but there's the obligation to continue in order to start "production" like they had advised at the hospital.

For the next two months, don't look down there I murmur to myself.

This is another thing one of the night nurses told me the first evening at the hospital. She was changing my underwear, carefully but also mechanically, the same way the gauze is removed from a wounded soldier, and she disposed of my blood-soaked pads without hesitation. The young woman knew something I didn't know, and I didn't even know her last name. I wanted her to lean over the bed, put a hand on my forehead, and reveal to me who had won the war.

Trust me she continued the speech about my vagina and paused, leaning over my pillow.

You don't want to know.

—

Later that night, it's meant to be my first bath after arriving home from the hospital, but John is the first one to use the shower while I'm nursing. Without a towel, he comes up to Button and me with the intention of planting kisses. His slim Adonis body reminds me of the body he had when we first met. He had the exact same physique with his signature chest hair that is as wide as my palm, dark blond and regularly trimmed. Now, resting my eyes at this clean figure, I am touched by jealousy. His beauty has remained intact during this whole time.

John has been a good man for as long as I have known him. The kind of good man who sorts out your retirement fund, sharpens your one good knife, and gets your shoes resoled as a romantic gesture. Someone who knows too much about merino wool and how to sew. Someone who orders vitamin D during the long winter and shares his bulk container of fish oil. It was a puzzle to me why he loved me. At the same time, it was the one thing that I couldn't allow myself to abandon.

And still, with the birth of Button, it was the death of John. I can't help but make it sound as though my husband is dead when I describe him. He may not be and of course he isn't, and yet and yet.

Right as he walks over to us, John's pink penis sways gently from side to side and I'm brought back to the time when the sight of his penis made me want to lie down with him, wherever: in bed, on the couch, on the floor. Here, it looks like a stranger staring at me in judgment, and the idea of doing any-thing with it feels as exciting to me as maneuvering a vacuum.

John leans down and kisses Button on the head as she is sucking on my nipple and, even though I am sure that he will kiss me next, the exchange of affection strikes me as unfair. His display of tenderness toward Button is a betrayal. I created Button, let me have your love first. At the same time, who am I to say anything? I don't wish to reciprocate. My body doesn't tingle after his every turn.

Your turn John says with buoyancy in his voice, smelling of warm water. I nod but stay silent and slip Button to him once she is groggy from the breast milk.

Behind the closed bathroom door, I run the bath and shake about a cup of Epsom salts out of the bag and into the water, swirling my hand around in the heat. I hang low over the tub. The water flows softly and unevenly between my fingers. Until I get back up again, I am only this movement. Free for a split second. The water slips from my fingers along with all my thoughts, making me think of the definition of "pacify."

While the hot water flows, I undress carefully. I'm not scared of the monster that presents itself in the mirror. I am scared of making a sudden movement in case the stitches will come undone, hips will pop. The body is in splinters. I'm too tired to bend over and clean blood off the bathroom floor. I still end up dripping over and into the tub. With that short step, I pass the small bin that holds all my discarded disposable pads, the leftover gore.

A slow, sad whimper comes from between my legs, strange vibrating pain. A part of me is trying to understand what it is that I have done, the rest of me is the wound. What have I done to deserve this? Who brought this state forward and how could I even begin to translate this madness?

I step in and in the water, I fold in half. With closed eyes, I hear myself louder than usual.

Please give me twenty minutes I gurgle toward the showerhead.

I tint the water around my legs light pink.

In the bathtub, I sit down and get moderately comfortable with my head leaning back on the edge of the tub. The heat from the water makes me anxious and sleepy at the same time. I'd like to relax. What could have possibly prepared me for this?

If only it was so easy as to cry.

Fuckedy fuck.

A sound shaped close to music materializes from above. Quite the melancholic tune, low and lingering; the neighbor's accordion from upstairs. With eyes still closed I put my hand in the water and snake it in between my legs. Short pricks of metal poke my fingertips. Stitches cover the inside lips of my vagina, lips so swollen I can barely open my labia, so I don't. After a couple days of not shaving, the carpet of hair is steadily growing back, perhaps wanting to cover up Button's exit.

It's not only my lips that are swollen. In the water, my body floats like a plastic bag filled with air on the surface. With my breasts large and the hair between my legs overgrown, I am more feminine than I have ever been before in my life. My belly, still bumpy, and my feet, still puffy with fluids.

Through the door, John tells me *We need you out here* and from this moment on I will never be alone.

In the immediate now, the music stops. I wonder who else heard it.

I will watch you too closely.

I will also love you because I am sure you will look more like your father than me. You will get his almond-shaped eyes and distinct nose. You will get my droopy eyelids and bad posture. Maybe you'll find a devotion and use my dictionaries as stools. Soon enough, you'll mirror my movements or expressions and frighten me with my own inadequacy. Just like today; I am reminded of my own failures.

I'm sitting at my desk on a simple fall afternoon, trying to focus on work with a subdued, almost wintry light shining through the window. The desk where I work is in our bedroom by the foot of our bed, nicely tucked away next to our dresser. Both the desk and the chair are doing their job. It's my mind that is wandering, making up different scenarios. I am growing impatient, my thoughts are fixated on your possible arrival. Since my period is late, I jump between it's happening, to it's going to happen, to it's happening, to what is happening. This is not the first time these thoughts have looped into each other, it's not the first time my period plays with me, but there is something different about this time around. My sense of taste is shifting ever so slightly.

The pages in front of me that I'm working on limit and suffo-

cate rather than exude play. The computer distracts, the clicking, the scrolling, the abyss of the internet. It doesn't help that
the apartment building is napping in movements and sounds,
as if digesting from a heavy lunch.

Then, as authors often frustratingly write in books and suddenly: a waterfall.

I stare out the window, waiting for something more, but it's
over before I have even understood what it was that happened.
Quick footsteps shuffle about upstairs. I walk over to the windowsill, unclick the two latches on the frame, and lift the window frame open with both hands. By letting the neighborhood
in, the room comes alive around me. It begins to breathe, and
I can hear people verbalizing their needs in different octaves
far away. At some corner there's even bickering, but it's hard to
tell if it's innocent.

I poke my head out and look up to the sky. A few drops
of water drip down the wall of the building and onto the fire
escape. From the upstairs window two hands appear holding
a planter. The plant is placed down and then the hands disappear. The leaves move, but only twice. The hand appears again,
and again it holds another plant. The small shrubs that are put
outside are lush and almost translucent with green leaves, they
are so alive. A long neck appears balancing a small round head
from which a short haircut dangles around the chin. What I am
observing at this moment seems natural and instinctive from
my neighbor's end. Here is someone intriguing. The woman
upstairs arranges her plants through few and determined
motions. She is wearing a cotton shirt, a watch, and a slender
ring, but no necklace. There's no fuss from the waist up as far
as I can see. Energetic tunes stream out from her apartment.

She disappears one last time and closes the window. The

music is muted. I'm left to watch the plants dangle lightly in the open air and wonder about her. The beauty of strangers, the beauty of other strange people. What kind of story could I possibly make up around what I just saw?

First I sit in silence of my shortcomings, then I return to my desk with slightly more patience than before.

At dinner, John tells me about recent articles that he has read: studies done about the connection between family wealth and real estate in this country, what the climate tech companies are doing next, and how the multibillionaires are trying to get their electric cars skyrocketed out to space. Button's latched on while I am eating with one hand. She seems all right for the moment. John's talking flows through me like a river and I am standing in the river, watching him and quietly eating takeaway pad thai. What do I have to contribute in this conversation? What can I give? I'm mostly thinking about my nipples, how they are sanded down to flesh from these first days of nursing.

Where are you? he asks.

Sorry, I'm tired.

I stare down at my plate.

This is yummy. Thanks for picking this up for us.

Aha he says and returns to his noodles. A silence bounces back and forth between us.

Some slow and sad bellows creep into the long pause of our conversation. I would have no clue as to what melody is playing upstairs, but I know that I like it. It's playing for Button.

Turning my head up toward our ceiling, I want to trace the sound with my eyes. All I can see, though, are a couple

of poorly patched holes, a silent smoke alarm, and a few shadows from the evening light of the apartment. John goes on to
explain that beef is the new coal.

I lean back into listening and the story of my poor nipples
stays with me. The bellows deepen.

Before the music disappears, I ask John

You really can't hear that?

What?

It's coming from upstairs.

Maybe you should lie down for a bit.

Button is eating from me, while I am myself eating.

Never mind.

A fracture forms in the ceiling and the music dies down. It
slowly ends. The rupture above us is subtle but already distinguished enough that I can tell it's something I will need to
address before it is too late.

The next morning, my senses are turned up. John's sandalwood
shaving cream still lingers in the apartment after he is gone. I
can smell Button from the other room, I can sense when the
fruit in the bowl is past prime, a fermenting tang emanates
through some bruised skin. I hear the flesh turning brown.
Oozing. A similar odor is coming from my body. I discreetly
check the nook of my armpit and it's obvious that I'm also a
couple of days past fresh.

Peter from upstairs sits by the dining table. He is sitting
quite naturally, resembling a part of a morning ritual, and I
forgot that I let him in in the first place.

He appears as a reliable man, yet still translucent in the
apartment. I go to the kitchen to fill two empty glasses with

water and when I set them down on the table, I have a feeling
that neither one of us will drink. Peter begins the portrait of
his wife.

There was a trip to do fieldwork and there was an accident
not too long ago. Peter received a call that his wife was in the
hospital. By the time he had arrived, she was in intensive care,
and the next day, he left the hospital with a plastic bag containing the last items that she wore. Strange how quickly time can
slip through your fingers.

As he lists the things she had with her when she died—a
pocketknife, a hand lens, a wedding ring, a dull pencil, a pair
of gloves—I go to the bedroom to scoop Button up from her
bassinet. I can't help but want to hold her while Peter is talking about death, and she lets me. When we come back into the
room, the list continues: a pair of hiking boots, pants, a long-
sleeved shirt, a watch with a leather band, a pair of reading
glasses . . .

No one mentions a bag.

He places his hands on top of each other on the dining table.

I walked out with the shell.

With Button moderately content in my arms, I tell Peter that
I am sorry and genuinely mean it. I ask him what it was that his
wife enjoyed about her work and maneuver Button onto my lap
on the couch. She continues to be a cooperative little bundle
and recoils into the background. I'm relieved that I don't have
to nurse her again, not quite yet, but that I can willingly have
her in my arms.

Her true love was moss.

Peter's words are spare until he warms up.

They're such a discreet plant, existing in plain sight and yet never asking for attention. Moss comforts, protects, and nourishes others—you can sleep on it, drink from it, stay warm. It's a very selfless plant, soft and lovable. Moss is also a landscape, expanding when you take your eyes off of it, appearing when you least expect it. Agata told him that moss could have both sexes and neither of them. And moss could never harm anyone. That's why they gave her so much pleasure.

Agata I say, and fold my eyes down to Button.

Her mother was Polish, but she was born not too far away. Up north. Closer to the woods than the city.

I resist asking what happened to his wife—how dangerous could a moss-examining field trip be?—but of course I want to know.

I imagine Agata falling from a mountain and unable to catch herself. I imagine her letting herself fall, I can't help it. Maybe she needed to fall.

Button stirs. Through my grasp, I can feel her intestines gurgling. A timer is about to go off.

She's about to explode.

I wanted these words to be delivered in the gentlest way, but Peter moves. Frazzled, he has forgotten that there was a baby here between us all along, someone with more straightforward needs. Button starts calling. Peter is clunky. He begins to retreat, he retreats. All three of us squirm from discomfort. What a waste of a day, and we were just getting started.

The door is closed behind him and I'm left with a foreign object. Peter's exit is quickly felt when he is gone, the air has stopped again in the room and I am faced with not knowing what to do

with us. The timer is ticking down faster. I think about how
when we clean Button in the evenings, her naked body (barely
a *she*) resembles store-bought poultry in my hands. So easy to
slice, but I shouldn't welcome the thought. Such vile imagination must be pushed out from my consciousness. Going back
to her skin, it is a soft and empty canvas, with the crust of the
umbilical cord at the center of her body still trying to hold on.

When John bathes her, I leave the room. Her nakedness also
exposes her small size. I can't handle the idea that she might
slip through his fingers like a bar of soap and fall to the floor
in one splat, yet the image loops and warps in my head. I may
soon have to acknowledge that I am losing my mind.

I mean, sometimes I picture myself crushing her with my
foot.

There comes that awful thought again, but this would mean
that the screaming will forever stop. I could go back to my
desk and no one would ever miss her. I would need to wipe off
the gunk from my foot, the slippery intestines, the soft skull,
the pinkish blood . . . I would place the fouled paper towel at the
bottom of the trash bin and go about my day.

Button is yelling in my face. My thoughts evaporate. Now
her screams hurt, because she is flushed. My breasts listen. Her
helplessness is particularly irksome today. But could I even
capture the moment when today began? After all, there is no
beginning and there is no end to this.

I decide to walk around the apartment in broken circles with
Button. The thought of Agata already feels like weeks ago. My
movements are not helping, she is still upset.

I put Button down on the changing pad, unwrap her, unbutton, unfold, tear the diaper open, pull wipes, wipe with the
wipes, grab a fresh diaper, and reposition it on her. Baby diaper

Velcro on the left hip, baby diaper Velcro on the right hip. I
button her crotch together and refold her into a bundle. I pick
her up and carry her around while I eat and shit and brush my
teeth. All the while, Button is an attachment. I put her down on
the floor but she struggles to relax, so I pick her up again and
try to lie down on the couch with her. Maybe I'm moving too
much. That makes her squeal. Maybe I'm moving too little. I
get up again and bob around for a bit in the middle of the living room. I don't even have a partner leading, but we do this
awkward dance for a while.

As I'm rocking up and down, from side to side, an image of a
large spider appears from around the corner of the ceiling. She
is like the giant *Maman,* a silent mother I can turn to. I can tell
by her heavy and calm movements. She stares at me knowing
that she has appeared because my mind asked for her.

Please weave me a bed I express over Button's cries. *Please make
this stop.*

The maternal spider motions her head to the side, she licks
her legs and starts spinning a delicate web from her asshole. It's
fine, soft work she is webbing in the corner of the ceiling. She
is dutiful. I am bouncing. Button is wailing with a flushed face.
I keep bouncing.

When the spider's work is done, she backs off, creeps around
some corner, and leaves the room. A silvery hammock remains
dangling in the air.

That's where I place Button, and I turn and walk away.
There is no more crying.

The silence that comes after putting Button down is tremen-
dous. It is as though a new sound envelopes me, created by air,

electricity, and what is left of my mind. The fridge hums, the noise machine steadily reverberates, the shower drips, and a signal goes off in my head.

In this newly brought forward stillness, I can taste time, and time tastes like my stale breath.

After all this, John comes home. Later than usual, which may explain the sighing.

This new deadline is killing me he says while taking off his leather shoes. He pushes a pair of cedar tree soles into each shoe.

I can't wait to be done with this project.

He goes to the kitchen sink to wash his hands, dragging another sigh along with him. He comes over to us with tenderness, smelling of traffic and grease, but mostly tenderness, and asks about his *ladies.* Nothing happened to us, did it? I mean, I guess that's the entire problem.

John lies down on the couch next to us and motions with his hands that he wants Button. She is in another post-milk haze with closed eyes and an open mouth.

It's endless I finally say. *The cycle is endless.*

I hand Button over to him. John squishes his face into Button's neck. He inhales. She is a passive, pink, little old creature.

Did you at least get some rest?

I tried I lie.

I want to collapse onto the couch but realize that I'm already sitting down. I stare into the open room.

What if you went outside?

John's suggestion is so random, the way strangers can stop you on the street to ask for directions.

I don't know where that is.

What?

He positions Button close to his chest without waking her up.

I mean, as soon as you leave, she needs something or a neighbor complains about her crying or there's someone dropping off a package.

There's always something.

They did tell us at the hospital that the first weeks will be the hardest.

John says this as if it's the simplest thing to say in the world.

Easy for them to state, but that doesn't help me. I'd like to walk away from us talking about this.

He ends the conversation with *Let me whip something quick together* for dinner and I am relieved as much as I am disappointed that he has already moved on.

The first meal I remember at the hospital was the most extraordinary dish I have ever tasted.

Someone knocked on the doorframe because there was no door attached to my room. A woman walked in without listening to a reply, wearing dark blue scrubs, and set a plastic tray down on a side table. In her movements, she was very matter-of-fact and wouldn't be someone who would stick around for a chat. The woman slid the table over my bed like an extended arm and lifted the plastic bell jar, then set it aside. Before leaving the room, she ticked my name off a list on a chart. I thanked her for the food.

I was expecting a meal three times its actual size, but what appeared as breakfast was three tired and flat pancakes stacked on top of one another, with a side of bacon. The meat resembled thin strips of leather instead of looking like it came from the edible part of the pork belly. A cold cup of orange juice sweated on the tray. It was covered in a metallic wrapping, and a serving of chocolate pudding kept it company. The presentation resembled airplane food, at least that's how John put it.

Are you really going to eat that? he asked.

With Button swaddled in his arms, John said he would go get us sandwiches or something, but I wasn't listening.

You don't understand I said without wanting to hurt him.

I must do this. I had to eat, and I ate and I devoured my plate as if I believed there was no tomorrow and I didn't even need to swallow because the inside of my mouth was slick with rows of fish scales, the food slid down effortlessly, and I drank everything, gulped and guzzled, leaving nothing edible on the tray. Even if my hunger was more animalistic than the bacon on my plate, I gnawed further life out of it.

At the sight of it all, John turned away, letting me do what I needed to do. He started rocking Button from side to side and I was fulfilled, for the moment.

The clock on the oven beams 11:03, it's evening. John has showered and has already shaved. He is cutting his toenails in the bathroom with the door closed, but the clippers snip through the air right past the door. The noise cuts into whatever romance is left in our marriage, which is not much since there is little of me to give to John right now, but I still feel obligated to get up and occupy myself with something.

In the background, while his electric toothbrush runs its course, I collect dishes that are scattered over the kitchen counter and dining table. I run them, one by one, under the faucet. The last traces of food slide off the plates and into the drain. I skip over the large knife in the sink. The dishwasher is almost full and I have to reposition some smaller bowls to make space for other ones.

Button is in a moving container, rocking back and forth in the middle of the room. She is wriggling but not making any noise. That means I have about ten minutes.

I collect greasy milk bottles and run them under the water with their innocently yellow lids. Perhaps there's still more space left in the dishwasher. Button utters an indistinguishable sound and raises a crooked arm. Does that mean she is verging on discontent? My chest expands from the worry and I wonder about how many minutes I may have left.

I throw away used paper towels and scrape off food from more plates. Our water glasses can be put to the side, we can use those again later. I wash a pot, a pan, and a few ladles. I wipe the countertops and the island and consider what the night has in store for me.

A fruit fly takes off above the sink and I follow it briefly in its swirling flight, thinking I could clap it dead but that might set Button off. I let the fly move freely around me. Maybe it's me it's searching for.

I can already hear Button. There's something that she wants and she is honest about it. Her body makes a low-grade wet-diaper cry and silence comes from John's toothbrushing. The silence lingers, then moves into his simple motions. He opens and closes the bathroom cabinet. He makes one last gurgling sound, one last spit, and when he opens the bathroom door the hot air from the shower changes the temperature of the living room. His clean scent contains sandalwood and hot water. The mixture of the two clouds up the apartment.

John has a sleepy bounce in his movements.

Your turn he says, passing on the invisible baton. I have to make a run for it before it is too late. He steps up to Button in all his nakedness and gazes at her from above. His back is still speckled with water and his blushing penis hangs unknowingly in front of her.

Button starts crying. It's the penis that has scared her, it would scare me too, but at her few days of age she still can't see very far. Yet from the warmth emanating from his naked body she must be able to tell that someone is near and standing over her smallness but not holding her.

Do you want me to pick her up while you shower? he asks, still looking at Button.

That would be nice.

I start taking off my clothes and hanging them on different pieces of furniture, leaving a tired trail behind me.

I think she needs a new diaper I add, moving toward the bathroom, slowly closing the door.

Button's cries turn up and I turn the shower on, attempting to drown out the sounds in the apartment. I unhook my unapologetically maternal bra and watch my nipples leak. Small see-through white droplets drip down to the floor; my body weeps after Button. Like a busted faucet, it's unstoppable and uncontrollable. I avoid my nudity in the mirror. I don't need a reflection to show me that my stomach is still stretched after Button's departure. The line that goes from my belly to my vagina is still long and dark, showing a path that makes little sense to me now.

I pull the shower curtain aside and step into the bathtub. I pull the curtain behind me and guess that I have four minutes.

In the wreck that is my body, the first wave of fatigue arrives. Though it is not quite distracting enough. In the living room, John is having a one-way conversation with Button, describing the things that he is doing and seeing. She makes noises regardless of and out of context to what he is saying.

When Button goes quiet, I'm curious if John has taken off her diaper. This may give me a few extra minutes.

I take all of the minutes and the shower is my one sole pleasure, though my body still belongs to Button and likes to remind me of that. But right now, the water is my companion. I let it drench me, I gulp it down, I stand in it, I fold over, I give in, almost tumble. Whatever it wants, I'll hand it over.

Reluctantly, I end up turning off the water and dully pat myself dry with a towel. A web of green veins extends across my chest. I clip the bra back on and brush my teeth. I notice some sticky gray marks on my back, remnants of the tape that held the epidural needle in place. I put lotions on my face, a gesture that is more of a joke, but I still hope for the best. I have no idea what is to come. My breasts have already swelled, tensing up to the pressure of new milk. Nipples tingle as if listening to a temperature shift in the room.

When I exit the bathroom, John is standing by the door with Button in his arms as if he has been listening in on me this whole time.

I think she's hungry again he indicates, because of course I have all the answers. He watches Button like she has told him something while I was taking a shower, but Button doesn't stare back to confirm or deny his statement, because she is a baby.

Let me get some water I say, and walk past them to the kitchen, meeting the oven again. It beams 11:17 at me and I grab a glass. While I fill it with water, I think of everything that could happen tonight. And yet, there is nothing that can prepare me.

I see the fire escape outside standing erect, empty of birds and plants. The metallic frame, a shadowy and gangly skeleton that holds on to the building in the dark, is more solid than ever.

Okay I say. *Give her to me.*

I google things in the night and these are the things:

hemoroids

search autocorrects

hemorrhoids symptoms
hemorrhoids treatment
constipation treatment
what is witch hazel
what is a bryophyte
what is gemmae
why do newborns spit up

Today I

How should I put this

I can't even feel that today is a day, like you do when you wake up in the morning and have removed yourself from the thought of the night. It's not about knowing what day it is, it's about having moved into a state of perpetual "giving," trans. *ger.* I'm living with a taker and her name is Button, still oblivious to a world around her, still a thing smelling her way forward. It's only what is immediately in front of her—my breasts, my skin, my warmth, my smell—that she wants to soak in.

Today started at 3:12 a.m., when I fed Button for an hour and held her for another hour and couldn't put her down because she would start crying.

Has there ever been a description of a mother holding her child for hours? Has anyone unraveled the little hours? My state might be a portrayal of the elasticity of time.

Now it is 5:25 a.m., and John is still sleeping soundly. In the dark nursery, we walk in infinity loops with the noise machine droning in the background. I can make out the contours of the furniture around us while I rock back and forth, forth and back. As recurring as a worshipper during the ritual prayer, I sway and sway. I squat. I tippy-toe and waltz with her—round and round—and sing the songs I know by heart and I hum them on repeat, sound them out in different melodies, and I'm still swaying and I'm still dancing and I can only go on for so long. She forces me to go on. So, I go on. I must go on. But from where do you pull more of yourself after you have given everything?

And yet you do, you do have more. From some core, you keep breathing. It is not the child that is at war with you, you are at war with yourself, and time is the referee. Unforgiving most times with the occasional mishap and vulnerable to persuasion.

I throw us down on the couch and we fall asleep and the night withdraws fully to the morning without us bearing witness to the transition.

A minute or an hour later, the alarm clock from the bedroom goes off and the artificial sound unnerves my tired mind. I almost forgot where I was. Outside, a garbage truck is making its morning round with unapologetic and ugly sounds.

Since Button is still in my arms and still quiet, I stay on the couch. I burrow us down and closer and farther, we are hibernating under blankets and pillows and through dazed eyes I follow John as he begins his morning routine. It reminds me of being at the theater, watching a performance of a one-man play. John turns on lights depending on which room he enters and leaves them on afterward. He dresses while eating breakfast; he addresses his audience on the couch.

I was reading that farmed shrimp emits four times the amount of greenhouse gas that beef does.

I am still hibernating. He buttons his shirt.

We need to stop eating shrimp he continues in between bites of milk-soaked high-fiber bran flakes. His spoon and his bowl make slight sounds when they meet and, soon enough, the morning melody also includes the spoon and the bowl being placed in the kitchen sink. John moves on in his routine and kisses me tenderly on the forehead. He strokes Button's head before he puts on his leather shoes. The pair of cedar shoe-tree inserts falls into a heap on the floor, making an uncomfortable clatter, but it's a short sound, Button and I can remain in our mild slumber.

Call me if there's anything John says, and closes the door behind him.

The play continues: one man exits the stage and another man enters.

Peter makes sounds in the hallway that I recognize even before he arrives at our door. The tank, his devoted follower, makes a slow and heavy thud, repeated each time it hits a step. I can hear them breathing in tandem, desperately reliant on each other. They're coming closer.

I will be opening the door for Peter. It's the only choice I can make.

From our cave-like condition on the couch I uncover Button and myself, she is fine and I am fine, I suppose, although I realize now that I'm pretty hungry. The blanket falls from us and we move to the kitchen. Button spits up on me and I reach for a towel as I try to decide what to eat. Here's his knock. Something quick will have to do.

With the kitchen towel thrown over my shoulder, Button tags along when I open the door and once I do, I return to feeding myself, after letting Button be in her container. I don't need to check to see who I am letting in. The strange couple trudges along and eventually comes inside.

We listen to a bowl of oatmeal spinning in the microwave. I can trace yesterday in my mouth and that reminds me, I am also thirsty. From the kitchen, I ask Peter what's going on. Slightly hunched over, he seems tired and lonely, even if he is among company. His shoulders appear a little damp, perhaps even moist, almost as if he had just walked out of someone's newly watered greenhouse, and the last gray hairs left on his head are flattened. Knowing his place in the apartment, he takes a few steps over to the dining table and sits down. He positions the tank next to the chair and twirls the tube around the handle, moving it to the side.

It's too quiet upstairs.

He glances at Button, perhaps with some concern that she'll start rumbling from her container.

Agata left many plants behind.

Peter believes they are growing frustrated from her absence and his neglect. They're becoming difficult to maintain. He waters them but can't keep up. He also forgets and waters them again. Maybe giving them too much. When I ask him if there is anyone who can help him with the plants or move them out, he mumbles something about not having had the chance to call her former students.

It seems as though Agata had the hardest time getting grant money for her research work. I suppose it makes sense when

Peter explains it to me. Moss is not exactly the sexiest subject. Many of the species don't even have everyday names because so few people consider them interesting or important. So they are usually called by their Latin names, something his wife believed made people even more reluctant to study them. In the evenings and after dinner together, Agata would run a bath for herself and, immersed in hot water, she listed the names she knew by heart.

> *Thuidium delicatulum*
> *Grimmia pilifera*
> *Hedwigia ciliata*
> *Bazzania trilobata*
> *Barbula fallax*

As if, when soaked in water, she was reciting a soft prayer. Continuing:

> *Dicranum fulvum*
> *Fissidens dubius*

The idea of her bath makes me envious. I tell Peter how lovely that sounds, *She seemed lovely,* and he slips into his native language by accident because what we are stating about his wife is so true.

Igen. He lets out a sigh only widowers can release.

The microwave beeps that it's finished and I press to open its door. My mind starts reeling from the hunger, my mind turns selfish.

I didn't bring anything for baby. Peter reminds me that it's customary to bring a gift when a child is born.

The oatmeal in the bowl has bubbled over. Goddamnit.

It's fine. I don't need anything from you I elaborate so nonchalantly. But what do I know. I just want to eat this bowl of oatmeal.

My comment makes him wheeze. I've offended the old man.

But of course I don't know what I'm saying. Avoiding the rest of this conversation, I try scooping the oatmeal back into the bowl. But of course I don't know what I am doing. I've yet to figure out where the limits are in this dynamic. What is being offered and what one should take from the other.

I apologize into the empty metal container even though the apology is meant for Peter and grab a paper towel to wipe the mess off the glass plate inside the microwave. I'm making things worse, spreading the sticky oats around, and my actions add to this pitiful state. Peter moves a pair of limbs to make himself ready to leave again, pushing the chair away from the table, and I hear something change: the walls shifted ever so slightly out of fear.

Instead of leaving, Peter puts a small glass container on the kitchen counter, I can't see where it came from, as if he pulled it out from his sleeve with magic or had it hidden behind the tank. Its presence in the room is a surprise.

One of her many *favorites* he says, and returns his hand to the tank.

While I spoon oatmeal into my mouth I see that the glass container is filled with a small, fresh, lush, green dome of moss.

Dicranum scoparium Peter injects into my silence. Or "mood moss," he adds, and says that I should keep an eye out for its emotions; when it has plenty of humidity it will grow fluffy and its color will stay bright, when the air is dry its aesthetics will resemble strands of hair. This odd but kind gesture makes me even more embarrassed over my previous comment. I want to hide in my bowl of oatmeal, I want to withdraw into the chores of domesticity, not be obligated to care for another living thing.

Na he says and gets up. Well then. He lets my silence linger.

Peter turns and walks carefully out the door, making his way back upstairs. I can hear each sluggish step and shuffle, his breath, step, and *gadunk*, breath and step and *gadunk*, repeated until he reaches and passes his door, which slowly opens and slowly closes. The stairway quiets. How many more times will he have the energy to come visit?

It's not fair I tell him.

John is rolling around on the couch, watching a skit on his phone from a children's show where a Muppet is dressed as a chef, claiming to be Swedish. John's got one hand down his pants and couldn't be more comfortable. I'm cleaning up after dinner, with a mind and throat filled with nausea and fatigue. My insides are redecorating to make room for a possible baby. I am on a boat and on the boat I am walking on a tightrope and on the tightrope I am drinking a gallon of water and the water tastes warm and a day old and I'm also expected to do the dishes, be a loyal wife, feel invested in my work. That's what's going on. My husband is entertaining himself at my expense and I would very much like to tip over and lie down.

It's spelled "pöpcørn" and he throws his head back again.

He's not even talking Swedish! I half-jokingly throw a kitchen towel at him.

But that's what makes it funny! Wait, watch this part with the microwave . . .

John points to the small screen. He bobs in his seat. I sit down next to him.

You just love making fun of me.

It's all right that he is making fun of me. I put my head in the curve of his neck. And for the rest of the night, John sings *börk, börk, börk.*

I am eating, but I am so tired that I miss the opening of my mouth and stab myself with a fork. I am so hungry that I sweat when I eat. A gifted sweet-potato casserole ends up on my lap, bits of cheese land on Button, who is of course in my arms. The mess makes me anxious like a madwoman. The mess debilitates. I consider throwing the plate across the room, but I am too hungry to spare an arm. My cheek hurts. I sit suffering.

I start eating with my hand. With the one that is not holding Button, I shove pieces of rubbery cheese and potato into my mouth, the buttery taste gives me instant pleasure. I am eating so fast I find it hard to breathe. The body would like to cry but I am too stubborn to let it. I can't stop and I can't stop myself.

Button nuzzles into the nook of my arm; she is searching for nourishment too. Unfazed by the movement and transaction, I give her a breast.

Now I am thirsty and this need must be fixed immediately.

Without me asking for one, John offers me a glass of water. He had been sitting in front of me all this time and I hadn't noticed. I even forgot how much I have missed him. He suggests something about being *kinder* to myself, plan *a little outing* with the baby. I bat his words away as my mind takes a selfish turn, and I guzzle down the water. Water has never tasted so good as after birth. I drink until my stomach hurts and water spills from the corners of my mouth. I swipe myself dry with the free hand before any water drips onto Button.

Button, who is steadily oblivious to everything. John, who is quietly observing me while he is taking his time finishing his plate.

The sleep that eventually comes to me is like a slap from an abusive husband. I don't recover from it and once I'm in it, I am in the vast Milky Way of sleep, the deep well of sleep, the bumper cars of sleep. While in bed next to a sleeping John and a half-swaddled Button, my dreams decide if I end up in a haunted house or in some surreal teacup, swirling around in a heap of pink-and-white ridiculousness with shimmering details. Similar to the time (last night or last week) I dreamed I was nursing a baby cheetah or gave birth to a basket of see-through baby chicks.

I'm being attacked by a stranger entering my house or it's Button, waking me with her cries. I want to keep a knife on my nightstand or a baseball bat next to my bed. I hear her and I grab my pistol from under the mattress. She fidgets and I am ready for the chokehold. It is not only the cries, though, every once in a while but throughout the night, Button moves and breathes as if she is still shocked to be out in the world. This is life and *living* cries through her tiny body. Air in her lungs surprises Button, she thinks she is about to fall backward, and my ears follow her every movement, deerlike and tender. I'm curious to know what she thinks she would fall into. Even in the dark, I keep my eyes out for life-threatening danger.

Right now, her cries call for feeding and my eyes have to adjust quickly to the complete darkness. Like some sloppy magician, she has unwrapped herself almost fully. I make out a line on her diaper. Button needs to be changed in the nursery before I do anything else and I swoop her up in a fumbled haze of sleep and sleepwalking and when I do, I see that she has also pooped. There's a murky milky fog around her waist. John remains asleep.

It is still dark when I carry her over to the changing table. The apartment lies in a bed of stillness.

For fear of waking Button fully, I don't turn on any lights and have to find my way through the shades of dark blue in the nursery. When I open her diaper, more darkness appears on her vulva and on the insides of her thighs. The creamy smell rises, shapes itself into a cloud and envelopes me. I move as swiftly as I can, pulling wipes, and maneuver her legs, but the more poop I wipe off of her the more it seems I'm spreading it around. The gooey texture is relentlessly stubborn. I keep wiping. I keep at it. Button is wailing with legs stretched out tensely. More wiping. My heartbeat is elevated, my mind is flushed. I'm unusually warm. John remains asleep.

Button conveys her unhappiness and I hear her. Deep into the night, all I do and am is to hear her.

You called for Miffo?

This thing that I feel, this state that I'm in, needs a name, and I remind myself that at the hospital, they tell you not to shake your baby. The internet echoes the same demand. Under no circumstance should you shake your baby.

Don't you dare shake your baby, Miffo.

After Button is clean and I have disposed of the soiled wipes in the monstrously hungry pail, I grab a clean diaper and package it around her waist. I put her miniature clothes back on and wrap her until she is a soft parcel. I lift her up above my head and her head flops over like a heavy tulip. She continues to wail.

Really, what harm could one shake do?

Google:

newborn sleep sacks
can swaddles kill your baby
how likely baby will die from swaddle
best swaddl methods
sleep deparievasion
can you die from sleep deprivation
can you die from a bleeding anus

Peter knocks a second time and it's the second time that I answer the door. I hesitated the first time, wondering how long this could go on even if I would like it to go on. He tells me the baby is crying. I thought we had been through this before. We have been through this before.

Today, my neighbor is more stooped over, with a gaze elsewhere rather than on us, carrying a pair of shoulders that are speckled with dust or sand or dirt, something. He smells like he has been outside, but I've never seen the man go past our apartment on the third floor. As if confronted by my own fears, I look at him more closely or for the first time. His eyes are clear blue, wrapped in circles and lines that extend into branches of wrinkles. He tilts his semi-bald head that's too big for his body, and his arms have grown longer since last time.

Peter has brought his reliable companion, and the oxygen tank is staring up at me like a suspiciously stiff toddler. I follow its clear tubing over to him and see how it snakes and divides and loops around under his nostrils and over his ears, behind his neck. Disappearing until it reappears to connect with the cylinder.

Button is curled up in my arm and clings to an exposed breast. I hadn't detected the wailing, how soft and steady it was, until Peter pointed it out. What had I been doing with my day before he showed up?

Can you make baby stop crying?

He explains that it's been over an hour and that's the first time I get a vague sense of time.

I can't sleep he says. *I need sleep.*

There's stubble on his face, whiteness speckled on his chin.

I try to ask him what he thinks it is that I should do since she is a baby, just an infant, I think to myself, from Latin "infantem," "in" as in before the ability to "fans," as in "speak," meaning baby won't do shit to help you out. I mean, should I forgive Button for all the harm that she is causing? Suddenly, I am not so sure.

My arms tighten around her, pushing the breast up to show cleavage. Peter grips the tank harder, whitening his knuckles.

Make the baby stop he reiterates.

Button quiets when I say Peter's name.

I'm not sure how to help you.

In broken English he says that he is not the one who needs help; we are having our first fight, and he doesn't need to tell me that I have brought this upon myself, but hearing it from a dying man doesn't help.

Perhaps you should leave I say, and with this statement I have ended the moment and rejected the possibility of getting out of my state. My last words reverberate around the apartment, shove rudeness along with them, and push Peter out into the hallway. His retreat is similar to a fearful burrowing animal's.

Before he is completely gone, a deep and uncomfortable set of movements transpires between us and makes me wonder if I will ever set foot outside of this building again. Instead, it's the walls of the apartment that move, taking one step closer toward me as the ceiling reverberates through shifty motions.

The door closes behind me and I consider throwing Button out the window. My body knows that my mind is not joking, but it also knows how to hold me back. She would land in our neglected courtyard, found perhaps only the next day or a week later, and that would be the end of this, but before I continue to entertain this dark thought there's a new knocking on the door. It's Peter again, verging on being relentless, adding to the unyielding cycle, keeping me from causing harm to the baby by his sheer presence.

I readjust Button in my arms and fling her over my shoulder. She relieves herself of small air bubbles. Curdled milk trickles down my upper back. I reach around and wipe a corner of her mouth with the edge of my robe. Covered in new stains and ready to apologize, I let my neighbor back in.

It must be sometime during the day because I am home alone with Button. She is paddling aimlessly in my arms, twitching, wincing, and John's at work with the freedom to think.

I unclick my bra, releasing the right breast, and it doesn't take long before Button smells her way up to the hill of milk. I watch her suck and suck and then swallow and swallow with gentle little probing lips and I watch the sucking for hours.

I watch her for hours, swallowing, and falling asleep, then sleeping, maneuvering, acting, wanting, getting and needing, and needing more. I watch her and there is nothing else in the world except me watching her and her eating from me, gulping down the moment. This is the moment. It is not pretty, I desire to lie down, she is still sucking and most of the time I just want to lie down and not have Button or John or either of them wanting anything from me, while she is still sucking, because I don't want to do anything again.

Nothing can get me to want to go outside, among people, plants, or animals, among cities or beaches, next to friends, acquaintances, and between rows of books, or clicking toward folders filled with manuscripts and invoices, paying for services, receiving receipts, printing, acknowledging, and accepting, but the option of abandonment doesn't exist either.

Does it, Miffo.

Breathe and suck. Because Button dies if I abandon her. And
I suppose I made a sort of silent agreement with John or life
that this Button should be kept alive, while she is still sucking
and while I still watch her suck. And while I watch, I think
about how the Swedish word *miffo* ('mɪ.fö) has been used to suggest a disability, someone always out of place, deriving from
missfoster, with *miss* being "missed" or "failed" and *foster* being
"fetus"—essentially, a monstrosity.

Someone buzzes from downstairs and interrupts my moody
thoughts with Button still in my arms. I walk up to the monitor
in the hallway and on the screen I see a guy in a baseball cap
with a label on his shirt that is unreadable. I don't recognize the
color of his company. Is this the moment when I let a violent
psychopath into my building? Does he carry sharp tools in the
box? Will he slice up Button before he comes for me? Primal
mother alarm kicks in.

Package for delivery the man says plainly.

Who is it for?

He looks at the cardboard box, turns it around a couple of
times, and reads the apartment number.

3R he confirms without looking into the camera.

Sir, what's the name on the package?

Through the monitor the guy makes the face of a flustered
man and tries to read the package again. He puts the emphasis
on the wrong syllable, sounds annoyed, eyes the door, head
tilted back, grips harder around the package.

I buzz him in.

His footsteps reverberate through the hallway. They're getting closer, making their way up to us. The man, too, is getting closer. With one tit out I stand ready to say goodbye to my life, but as soon as I open the door there's a thud and the man is running back down before I get to face him.

In the stupid stillness that follows, alone again with Button and unsure of what to do, moments from the past appear, sweep in like a surprising breeze, stay like the droning of the air conditioner.

I'm in the grass, behind a church, with a tall lanky boy who has a chipped front tooth, and we're about to kiss but my phone rings and it's my parents and I answer and my phone is as big as a bus. Something's up, my mother is dead, there's been a terrible accident and I remember dragging a sweaty hand across my thigh to dry it on my jeans. The boy is disappointed by the interruption. I find it all very strange; I had just seen my mother. She was very much alive as she stood in the kitchen, waving through the window as I was leaving to meet the boy. When I get home, the house is silent as though nobody is there. One candle is lit on the dining room table and the rest of my family is sitting around the solemn light. I go to the bathroom and find a shiny wet spot on my underwear. I can smell the boy's breath on my face. I touch the bristles of my mother's toothbrush and it is still damp. The next day at school the boy calls me out for abandoning him with his erection. *Tjenare Miffo.* Classmates are amused that they have a new nickname for me. "Hey, how you doing, Miffo," and I go mute for an entire month.

In another moment, I am eating from a bowl of my mother's sweet peas. I am sitting on a horse without a saddle. I am making mixtapes, writing down the song titles on the insert. I am walking across a pair of abandoned train tracks. I am riding a bicycle without a helmet along an endless field of rapeseed. I am waiting in line at the post office. I am waiting for the train to arrive and I am reading a book while I am waiting at the station. The book has been given to me by a boy who I slip notes to in between classes. Different boy from before. A reply from him is my bookmark. I'm biting off my purple nail polish while in class. I am calling in to a radio station to request my favorite song. I sit and wait patiently with a clean cassette to record, trying to push the red button fast enough when my name gets mentioned on air. I eat frozen dinners. I return to my room.

I am often a teenager.

I gave birth and birth made me into a child. Button was out of me, I turned to the side, and my legs curled up in a fetal position. Never have I wanted my own mother so much.

Maybe twenty minutes have passed, it's difficult to know with all the sucking and the thinking and the devoid of thinking, and it doesn't matter if I make a note of where we are in the day because I am bound by Button. Without her knowing, I go back in time again and again and spend the afternoon at the local library or I make the walk I always made from the train station back to my childhood house and watch the sky turn from blue to an almost white, to lilac to pink, before the memory disappears completely and I am still in the exact same spot as I started out with Button. Except now she needs a new diaper and there's no childhood house to return to.

Has there ever been a description in literature of what it entails to change an infant's diaper?

The horror of mundanity. I have yet to find the appropriate translation of the experience, but I am compelled to try. Where is the accordion to wash me out?

Peter's absence is felt in its entirety. When he is not here, I find myself aiming my thoughts and worries at him anyway.

It's been a long day for the both of us. On his way home from work, John has brought back takeaway and the kitchen counter quickly becomes covered in plastic bags, containers, wrappers, utensils. The apartment smells of grease and salt, signaling that we are tired, lazy, and hungry. I've been getting away with taking extra naps at home but no matter how much I rest, the body asks for more.

The satisfaction from the food is immediate, and we leave large chunks of our conversation for later, when we have more energy. John opens a bottle of red wine with dinner and I pretend to drink from my glass the entire night. How cute of me to pull out some theatrical moves to distract him and how sweet of him to let me without mentioning the obvious. The obvious is that I haven't told him about you yet.

Let's digest on the couch. John wipes his mouth.

Okay I say simply and very much in love.

We leave our dirty plates on the dining table and slump down on the couch.

Before John sits down next to me, he turns on a pair of speakers that stand on the opposite wall to the couch. He scrolls through his phone and starts a playlist, dims the lights. He gets comfortable, sits down next to me, and exhales deeply.

I'm so full.

He sounds tipsy. I hum in agreement.

The music emanating from the speakers comforts. It's play-ful but not the kind of tunes that ask us to jump to our feet. We sit here, blend into the couch, and hang out, *myser.* I think of what everyone else is doing in the building, in their small individual cells.

This is so nice.

I coil into the nook of his arm.

He sits with eyes closed, exhales agreeingly with his head resting on mine, and this is one night of many spent alone together on our simple couch, in our simple apartment, in the midst of living our simplest, most meaningless lives. This was before I understood that it was this exact simplicity that would be taken away from me.

Today, like yesterday, so let's call it tomorrow, Button is latched on and is sucking and snoozing in a tender rhythmic loop. We are sitting on the couch in the living room and we are home alone. I can feel my stitches while sitting, small stabbings between my legs. The light from outside is muted and kind. I look out the window and see three brown doves perched on our fire escape. One is larger than the two others, which have softer, fluffier feathers. It must be a mother with her baby dove chicks.

Mama dove by the window is observing me with tender seriousness. I watch and ask myself if she is my neighbor. This is the first time I see her around. The bird's head tilts, and her babies are bumbling around on the ledge with an ambiguous expression on their beaks.

Mama dove is perceptive, she is understanding of my state and that's why she is here. She is here to support me and as soon as I feel nurtured by that thought, she is gone. Her babies start speculating when she will return. Their chirps quickly turn worrisome. I think of how lovely the word "dove" is: *douve, dufe, dubon, dufa* to be *duva*. "You" also begins with "du" in Swedish, reminding me of "diving," "nosediving," "submerging."

Before Button falls asleep, I switch positions and let her lean over my shoulder. I massage her back in slow circles and return my gaze out the window. How unhesitant mama dove was when she flew away. How tempted I am to do the same.

The golden hour has hit the opposite building and a flushed light reflects off the walls. Bundles of cables hang in frantic formations. I sit and watch. We are both breathing and are of the moment. It is all we are, and I'm tempted to admit that it is quite pretty, even for a mess.

There is a world outside of this apartment and I recognize that there is lots going on beyond this room. The act of breathing, sleeping, eating, shitting, are all insignificant to most, and still Button and I have entered into a dance, a kind of survival tango where we are clunky and at our most vulnerable.

There is no detaching from this.

When she sucks: I smell of milk, I am of milk, I am milk.

The blanket of milk, the cloud of milk, the waterfall of milk, I am of it. The drop of milk, the trail of milk, the running, the stream, again. I am the free-flowing fluid.

Milk is on my skin, its residue around my nipples, dried under my breast, wet under my armpit, or milk rests in day-old sweat. Milk on my clothes, behind my shoulder, or in a slow dried landfall down my chest.

Milk breath. Milk remnants, like cottage cheese, linger on me. Milk finds all my nooks.

When am I ever really clean anymore?

Milk notions, milk supply and her demand. The idea of drinking milk from another animal has now turned grotesque and intriguing, an odd pair of emotions left for me to handle. I can't get away from the sweetness of my own. And she likes it.

—

Of all the words I know in two languages, "milk" is the one I have memorized in multitudes: *mjölk, mælk, melk, milch, molokó, mleko, lac, latte, leche, gála; tej* in Hungarian, *süt* in Turkish.

There's the accordion, Peter is playing upstairs. A slow, dragged-out tune that makes me think of communism, bread and oranges, liquor and ill-fitted tights with the occasional hole. I don't really know anything about my upstairs neighbor. What should I do with this possible connection? Does he find my thoughts vile? I don't know if any judgment has been placed on me. As gullible as any lovestruck girl, I find myself hoping that he will come visit again. May he have the strength to keep coming downstairs.

Once a little burst of air has escaped Button's body, I cradle her again. She is not even as big as the pillow next to us.

What if the pillow somehow lands on top and suffocates her? What if, in my postpartum delirium, I accidentally place her down on her stomach in the bassinet and she dies? What if I one day step on her? What if I do anything to her with intention? What if I let her sleep for too long and she dies smothered by my embrace? What if there is a day when she simply stops breathing? With or without my intention.

Questions are the most banal, *ban, banel, bannan, banana, bananas,* and I see spit on my shoulder, already soaked in.

For distraction, I check my email on the phone and immediately regret it. Filling my inbox are unread messages in two digits, soon creeping up to three. Editors asking me when I can be scheduled again for translations. "Schedule"—what an ugly word.

Some send along a manuscript for me to "have a quick look." There are a few congratulations, some spam emails. The occasional remittance advice for delivered work. The occasional nonprofit newsletter. I'm not sure what I was hoping to find in my inbox. The phone is the least comforting device, a subtle parasite.

The accordion continues with the soundtrack of melancholy. The room swells and deflates around me. Soon enough, I will turn into the four walls, align my spine in all corners. Peter will place a hand on my shoulder. He will listen.

How do you schedule a piece of splinter?

I used to be a translator and now I am a milk bar. Both are quite solitary jobs and I can't say that I've ever been much of a people person, that's why the work of a translator suits me. I don't mind standing in someone's shadow. There's a kind of masturbatory pleasure in producing a book that others can read and find enjoyment from on their own without the pressure to produce the original. However much I have wanted to produce something separate from someone else. And if a mother's work is mostly work that is unseen, then translating is perhaps more mother-like than I have given it credit for in the past.

Between the immediate past and the torturous present, I find myself retreating behind my words. There are a handful I repeat to John when he is at home, but after *Give her to me* and *Can you take her for a sec?* how can I explain to him what is going on? How could anyone understand? The simple fact is that I am home alone with a baby all day. *Jag är hemma med en bebis hela dagen lång.* I'm not even sitting in solitude at my desk but standing in the middle of four walls, holding but barely holding on. Women have done this before me and nothing changed. And women will do this after me. Perhaps nothing will change.

This concept can't be literature.

I give up ruminating over these questions and put my face in the neck of Button. I inhale the scent of her buttery skin and sit in the cloud of her smell until she needs me again.

Something's off in the air. We're off. I'm on my hands and knees.

What are you doing? John asks while he is cleaning up after dinner, wiping the kitchen counters. I was nursing Button but I forgot about the unusual gift from Peter that was out in the open and I'm trying to hide the glass jar of moss under the couch.

I'm just . . . moving this jar.

What are you talking about?

A neighbor gave it to me.

Which one? You don't see anyone. John is filling the dishwasher, avoiding my eyes or on the verge of having had enough of me.

The old man from upstairs, whose wife was a botanist. I've told you about him.

John is inspecting me. I can see him thinking, contemplating whether or not he should pick a fight with me.

You mean a bryologist?

You know what I mean.

Whatever—I don't remember you telling me about him.

He continues with the dishwasher as if it's really the dishwasher he is having this conversation with. He explains that what I'm doing doesn't seem quite right, it's not normal to not meet anyone, to be *cooped up* like this, to act so strange, to not see people—it can go on only for so long. He is trying to make me aware of the world outside our apartment. There is more to this than *this*. I avoid his statements but understand his irritation. John must have had a hard day. Too many back-to-back meetings at the office and I don't entirely mean that in an insulting way.

It hasn't been that long I lie while climbing back up onto the couch to reattach Button.

John doesn't fully soften his demeanor.

It sucks that I have to work all the time. That's all.

And you seem different he adds.

Well, I am different.

He comes up to us and takes Button out of my arms. Resembling the item that she is, the little baton is passed on, but it hurts to get unlatched.

Hey, I don't think she was finished I say, and Button starts to cry and cries and John holds her almost an arm's length away and I notice small drops of milk leaking down to my stomach. I want to fight him, peck the man to death as if we were in a cockfight. But you can't take a woman with her tits out seriously.

John drops Button down into my arms before I can get to him and that's the end of us talking for the rest of the night. I want to walk out on both of them, step out through the window and climb down from the fire escape. Let them find me by the trail of spilled milk I leave behind.

John goes to get ready for bed, the sounds of his evening rituals give it away. I stay and sit with Button and I stay and sit with Button and stay until John has fallen asleep and once he has fallen asleep I leave both of them and drag myself over to the couch, still fuming with anger. I bend down low again, pick up the glass jar of moss from under the couch, consider hurling it all the way to the bedroom, only to get John's attention, but instead I get up to place it on the windowsill, having no idea what this plant needs. Fatigue makes these emotions fizzle too early and I try to rest until it's time again to abide by Button.

I am always the mother to my child, but sometimes I suppose I forget that John is the father to mine.

They feed you and then they disappear. Even John leaves so he can sleep more comfortably at home. A clock on the wall makes time so glaringly obvious.

As the first night in the hospital unfolds, a hazy blue layer settles in front of my eyes. The lights are out, but you can still see light coming from the corridor, light coming from the buttons on your bed, light coming from the obscure world outside. It's as if they have set up the room for the illusion of nighttime, which makes resting difficult, but it's because you are expected to be available whenever the baby needs you. Thankfully, Button doesn't need me right now. She is sleeping in a thick cotton cocoon in the hospital bassinet next to my bed.

Roughly every two hours some small event happens, my vitals are checked, the catheter is plucked before I have the chance to let out a scream, but there is nothing that is in my control. The night nurse introduces herself to me, writes her name on a whiteboard at the foot of my bed, and checks my pain medication. She is happy to give me more if I'd like more and I give in to her suggestion. I also let her take me to the toilet. I let her patch me back up before letting me get comfortable in bed. I let her fill up my water bottle. *Sure, ice would be nice.* I let her leave me an odd-looking chocolate-nut bar next to my bed.

Thank you I let out. I let her fluff my pillows. I let her put socks on my feet. *Thanks so much.* I let her show me which buttons to push if I ever need anything else. The button that looks like a person with a square hat is her. *Thank you again.* As one final thing, she suggests taking Button out of my room so I can get some sleep and I let her. The night nurse calmly rolls her out.

The whiteboard says "Meg."

As soon as they leave the room, I miss them tremendously and I regret not proposing to the night nurse. I tell myself that next time she comes back I'll give her many more loud and clear *Thank you*s. I'll ask her if she has any kids, or maybe that's too direct. I'll ask her how long she's been at this hospital. We'll take it from there. And depending on how that conversation goes, I'll ask her to run away with me before dawn comes. She can continue to tend to my wounds as we drive away, and I'll try to be good to her, faithful, lead the way.

After I've decided on my plan I see that only a minute or so has passed and she won't be back for another couple of hours, neither will Button unless I call on her. I'm too scared to call. She'll think I'm crazy. I browse the different shadows and reflections in the room, spot a tiny version of myself in the dark TV screen at the top of the wall. I think I fall asleep because when I check the clock again maybe twenty minutes have passed but I don't feel rested at all, my mind has been spinning all this time. I look for the remote that's tied to the bed and I press the person with the square hat. I hear it ringing.

This is Meg.

Can I please have my baby?

The night nurse asks if everything is okay, the baby is sleeping now so I don't need to worry, I should sleep, too, but I want her to bring me my baby, I beg her to bring me my baby. *Please can I have my baby.* She should be able to hear that I am crying, I hope she can hear me crying, and some minutes later, they roll my baby back. After this point, Button never leaves my side and a dance of desperation, confusion, and exhaustion continues throughout the night.

Are you sure you won't come with? John is strapping Button to his chest. There are so many tiny little things dangling from him and other things that need accommodation—a hat for the noggin, sleeves that protect her from her sharp fingernails, a spit-up cloth, a blanket, and the separate bag that can serve for any accidents. I stand by, clicking Button in, covering and folding, tucking and arranging so they can get ready to be on their way.

It's important for you to meet the pediatrician he says like a dutiful parent.

Button's first checkup is today, where they weigh and measure her to see if she fits into the parameters of healthy. I just won't be joining them. The walls around me stand tensely erect, the corners hold on, and the crack has hooked itself onto my robe.

I could use some sleep I say to John and pat his chest. I stroke Button's head and try not to lie too much.

All right he gives in.

And these are the things you want me to pick up at the drugstore? John holds up a Post-it note with my scribbles, unsure of what purpose some of the items serve. Well, this brand of stool softener is a given and affirms the notion that marriage is about the many unspoken but assumed factors between two people. But afterward John has to head back to the office. John is technically sacrificing his lunch hour for this.

I appreciate it I say and can't wait to withdraw.

I close the opening of my robe and retie the belt around my waist.

Okay, wish us luck! John kisses me quickly. They head out the door and I hear him talking to Button as they make their way down the stairs. She is his *sweetie* and together they're off on an *adventure*. Good luck.

The door closes and I am hit with the feeling of failure. It is immediate and gut-wrenching. I am an amputated soldier without Button and want to run out into the line of fire to catch up with them. However, my failure is also suffocating, vengeful and swollen with malicious intent that keeps me locked within the walls of the apartment, as invisible as an electric fence for dogs. This is cowardice. I can't escape even if I wanted to.

I go and collapse onto the bed. I go somewhere far away, beyond walls and words. If I want to be anywhere else, I can be found lying in the grass on a big open meadow. I am walking around a sculpture in a sculpture garden. I am wandering through the halls of a library, touching the spines of books, smelling the paper, flicking a light switch. Time is on my side, hiding in the background, minding its own business. Time is the man riding the lawn mower at the other side of the meadow. It is the woman handing me my ticket at the entrance to the sculpture garden. It is the student with their head in the books three rows up in the reading room.

Is this the time to reunite with my mother? Should I do everything I can to be with her again?

To be mothered is my strongest wish, but, I suppose, sleeping is care enough.

When I wake, my breasts have molded into a pair of bags filled with pebbles embedded under tissue. Together they are stabbing me from the inside out.

In a tired form of desperation, I undress from the top up and hook myself to the breast pump. The release comes slowly and painfully as the milk flows into the two separate tubes, eventually into each bottle. Science fiction is happening right in front of me, but the event is too painful to witness. I have to massage and stroke myself in order to find relief. I may pass out again, the agony in my chest is so striking. Fifteen minutes later I stumble back into bed.

When John comes home, I hear his steps are springy even though Button is howling. She must be hungry. There are so many parts to unclick and unwrap and untangle for John to separate himself from her. There is minor grunting involved. He fumbles like a new parent but doesn't seem to mind too much. I'm not sure how long they've been away, but it's clear my body can't take it without her anymore and the temperature rises.

All good he pronounces as he comes into the bedroom and John hands her over to me in bed like a trophy. Together they smell of fresh air. I sit up and pull my clothes aside.

Although the pediatrician asked for you. Said it's important for the mom to be at these checkups.

Fine I say.

Next time I say.

Good he replies. And John adds that apparently we need to call the hospital to get the full medical records sent over to the pediatrician, they still haven't received the paperwork. He holds an unbearable lightness around these new responsibilities we have, whereas I sense dread over these duties and how I eventually will need to leave the apartment. I want to stay in bed. This is my piece of land that I would sacrifice blood to protect.

Together we watch Button eagerly sniff her way to the hill of milk.

I was worried they thought I had stolen the baby John admits with a side smile and goes back into the hallway. He grabs a heavy plastic bag and heads to the bathroom. He puts my drugstore items in the cabinet underneath the sink and I thank him from the bedroom, but he is already on to other things. The man is living his life; contemplates out loud about making a smoothie for himself. Instead he grabs a nut bar from the cabinet and heads back into the office to make up for lost time.

I stay in bed with Button. This time around, I must have slept through Peter's knocking.

John is at work—the husband is away, the child needs to be held, and I need to go to the bathroom, but who cares about the needs of the mother, about *mina behov.*

In the living room, Button is latched on and I have to poop. It's not a hold-it-in kind of moment. It's going to happen with or without my wishes. I can't unlatch Button and I can't not take this shit. It suddenly feels hot in here. The walls are sweating, the air stands tall, sharp corners press against my temples. I have to go so badly I may throw up. My hips are shaking.

I bring her with me to the bathroom and peel my pants off while I hold her with one arm. The mesh underwear gets caught and I have to tear it, otherwise I will shit down my leg. I would like to not shit down my leg. A pressure pushes on my anus. Button struggles even if I'm the one doing all the work, and she is visibly upset, fuming with red because I'm not rocking her. I manage to sit down on the toilet together with her in my lap and with the release I can tell that my upper lip holds little beads of sweat. I taste salty. My stomach relaxes.

Thank goodness for the release, the fall, the stillness. Goose bumps appear on my arms, my body needed this so.

—

Before I can gather myself, someone knocks on the door. It must be.

It is as if Peter can smell my vulnerability. What a tortured state to find me in. And yet, I am relieved that he is back.

I wrangle with the toilet paper and hold on to Button and grab a new pad and lift a pair of underwear from underneath the sink and wonder if there's a place in the world where I can go to show off these new acrobatic skills. Before I wash my hands, I have to put Button down on the floor however much resistance she may give me.

You'll be all right, right?

She tells me otherwise while I'm drying my hands.

In the mirror, I see Miffo again, looking desperate, but there's another knock and I don't have enough time to go into more detail of that thought.

This package is your husband's Peter says, standing by the door, certainly not one for hellos. He hands over a padded envelope, explaining how someone dropped it off to him by accident.

I thank him and take the package. I place it on the kitchen counter with my free hand since Button comes with me wherever I go. In this unremarkable interaction, I have one of those rare moments when you know that something is going to happen with the person you're right in front of. Wherever we go from here, it will shape everything. Food will either taste sweeter or we will lose our appetites, but it is not going to be the same ever again.

Do you want to come in?

A moment later and as if to immediately confirm this feeling, I am "entertaining" Peter in our living room. My body is as light as a feather after relieving myself, and he sits down at our dining table with a forward-leaning posture as if he is getting himself ready to talk.

There's a little bend in his back and slight movement in his fingers. I am fidgeting around the apartment because sitting down in front of him would make everything we say much more loaded. I hope it doesn't smell in here.

I turn to the kitchen and decide to make us tea while he settles into his seat, pulling his tank to the side of the chair.

I heard you pacing he says. Peter's words are weighted equally as a question or a statement. He says I was moaning like some injured creature in the dark the night that Button arrived.

What were you thinking of? Peter speaks so faintly I'm scared he may be a ghost.

Standing behind him by our kitchen cabinets, I can observe his body without judgment. There's something about his crumbling posture that takes the pressure off mine. I grab a cup for him and fill it with water. I squeeze Button a little closer and it seems like she has nodded off; that relaxes me some.

You mean at the time?

I place the cup in the microwave, press the beepy buttons, and watch the plate inside begin to spin.

At the end.

The microwave dings. Time is as faint as Peter.

I take the cup of hot water out of the microwave and place it on the counter. I tear open a teabag with my mouth and let the thin little satchel sink into the water, watching it turn into a beverage.

I guess I thought I wasn't ready.

As if I had suddenly made the biggest mistake of my life.

He lets me go on. I put the cup in front of him and get a hint of his scent, earthy and fresh, like a recently fallen log in a forest. He nods a little thank-you for the beverage and I still can't get myself to sit down in front of him. Instead, I start a little bobbing dance in the living room, pretending that Button needs more convincing to stay asleep.

Not that my life was so remarkable before I indicate, turned away from him. But this wasn't what I had expected.

The night that she came out, I kept thinking that I wanted her to stay in. I wasn't ready to mourn the life I was leaving behind.

Before, I was alone and there was no one to tell me that was a problem. John wasn't even bothered by it because he had accepted that it was part of my job. Before, I would sit in front of a desk for several hours straight each day, scratching my head. I would move words around in almost endless variations, carve out a sentence or two, and occasionally dive into deep internet rabbit holes or argue with a colleague about if there is such a thing as a "faithful" translation. Other than one or two deadlines per year, no one was expecting anything else from me.

Before, I had rituals. Before, there was the luxury of getting lost on my walks. Before, there was the wandering of the mind. Before, there wasn't the cliché "You don't know what you've got until it's gone."

Before, I could spend time staring at letters. Before, I could choose between this word or that and settle on the third option, linger in the silence. Before, I could hide at the library. Remember libraries? The one place where no one asks anything from you.

Before, I could drink a cup of coffee and only be drinking that cup of coffee. Sometimes I wouldn't talk to anyone the entire day until John came home. The work was solitary, but it was never isolating. Was it all meaningless? I can't bring myself to think that it was, and is the arrival of a baby any more meaningful? All I know is that the stillness wasn't aching before. There was more peace, there was more control, there was more independence, *självständighet*—the self capable of standing steady on their own.

There is nobody to teach you that motherhood is forever, so how is it not a shock to your system when you find out that it is, in fact, until forever? How can this even be called motherhood?

I want to explain to Peter that this is not a complaint. At the same time, there's no avoiding that I'm objecting to the state I've placed myself in. If that means that I am myself to blame then I am myself to blame.

The fundamentals lie in motherhood, that is why it is vilified.

Maybe the baby asks you to submit Peter implies by the time we come to the end of my venting, and we both decide to look at Button. She can't even see us and has no idea who the person holding her is or what they are capable of. I haven't even figured out what I am capable of.

The three of us sit like this and we sit like this because we are convinced there is nowhere else for us to go.

John and I are having dinner and he is feeding Button a bottle so I can finish eating. We tried to have sex last night. We were on top of each other in bed like stacked cardboard and lasted for maybe five minutes. The only thing that I felt was the slow rhythmic jerks of our machinery. I smelled his slightly sandalwood-scented skin. The rest of me was empty. There is little to say and in this instance it is difficult to place us in relation to time. Though I had gotten the "clearance" on sex from the doctor to indicate the passing of our days and weeks, it still wasn't that long since Button's birth. That's exactly how malleable time is after giving birth—the body is equally malleable, I suppose.

At the dinner table and in between bites, sitting newly showered in my robe, I want to explain to John how, for a short while, I was an empty box. When we were in bed, and he was on top of me, I imagined I was holding the box that I was and the act of sex was me holding said box.

And you were just a penis.

John is listening.

This rod.

He can't help himself from smiling.

Stop laughing, I'm serious.

Okay okay. He nods.

John is trying to maneuver the bottle and the cradling while I'm trying to describe an act he was also present for. He attempts to contribute to the conversation.

You remember my first roommate in the city? He smiles gently. *You know, she got pregnant soon after she met her boyfriend, that really nice carpenter guy. I remember her saying that sex after giving birth is like throwing a sausage down a hallway.* He starts to chuckle and goes for a bite of food on his fork. I watch and wait for a piece of spinach to land on Button's chest, almost astonished by what he just told me.

Thanks.

Button bounces with him as he is laughing.

I always thought that was a funny way to describe it he says, and keeps on chewing.

I get it I say.

I take off my robe and leave it passive-aggressively on the floor.

But anyway, don't worry he adds after I've already left the table. *Your body will bounce back.*

I can't stand that everything John says is a quote, a handful of scripted words that are easy to say for the sake of saying something. I play out an entire fight between us in my head and watch myself shout the filthiest words I know at John. I see him crying at the end, which is exactly what I'm aiming for. This rage doesn't understand proportions, but, like me, it is also a coward, it gives up too quickly and folds into sadness. It's equally as tired as I am, and I can't even go back to show him my disappointment.

—

That night, John's sound sleeping is particularly maddening. In bed, surrounded by blue darkness, with him next to me and Button all the way in the next room, I can sense the pressure of the air in the entire space. My desk stands in the corner, solidly waiting, obviously neglected. The spine of the new novel I'm meant to translate is not even cracked, it's collecting dust. I may be the only one awake in the apartment building. Alone I conjure up faint memories of Peter's accordion, make the dead keys ring through again, and wish my neighbor was still alive to keep playing them. The bellows expand slowly, releasing sighs of deep comfort. Anyone else listening would be lulled into sleep by the instrument's long and slow breathing. Soft images appear: a boat gliding into its dock; a city waking in the morning; a wind blowing through an empty field.

I see the ceiling opening up and me rising to lie on the floor above. The ceiling closes under me. I have my eyes closed to the lullaby that hums in the background. I grant myself permission to do nothing—blissful nothing—and I can sleep if I want to, rest if I want to, I do very much want to. But Button

Here she goes.

She needs me again so I spoon her up in my arms and take her to the couch in the living room. On the way, I pick up my robe from the floor and envelop us.

We sit down and it comes as a surprise that I'm not hungry or thirsty at this moment. I cover us in a wool blanket and feel its immediate heat. Should I go ahead and smother her and pretend it was an accident?

I pick up a pillow to place it behind my back but instead I pick up a pillow and place it on top of Button and on top of that pillow I rest my head and with my head on the pillow I close my eyes and lie still, very still.

In this dream, I have killed her, but here, we have fallen asleep.

The tune of the accordion is the murmuring of the fridge, the buzzing of the digital oven clock, the faint street noises from outside the building, the stagnant air inside the apartment. By now, it's a song I know by heart.

In our awkward dark nest, between sleep and wakefulness, I unwrap Button and start grooming her. I can't see what color it is, but from the softness of the material I can tell that it's lint that I find in between her fingers. I take my time examining, feeling my way. She reminds me of a combination of all the animals that I have ever seen. She has the skin of a see-through rabbit, the swollen eyes of a puppy, the tiny whimpers of a kitten. I should be resting and here I am again, churning. Snotting. Whimpering. Mothering?

Barely.

Kära Mamma. My dear mother, I can't believe you are not here.

I scoop wax out of her ears, soft like beeswax, but when I smear it between my fingers it disappears, leaving a slightly oily touch. I nibble on her fingernails; they taste soft, flavorless. I bite them off one small, filmy, and chewed-through piece at a time. I scrape flakes of skin off her feet. I wipe curdled milk from her many nooks. I gnaw on this body that John and I have created, but I do no harm. Maybe tomorrow I'll try to talk to him.

Miffo?

Are you there, Miffo?

The room doesn't reply, and Button passes gas.

Google:

flange fit options
how do you know your flanges are the right size
how do you know your breast flanges are correct
what is a flange
why would a mother want to kill her baby
how common is wanting to kill your baby

Peter places one hand on the cup of tea, leaving the other hand on his thigh. The oxygen tank is next to his chair. If the building moved and the floors shook, it would tilt and the tank would probably crush Button if she were lying on the floor. And yet, she is not on the floor and the tank is standing sturdy and this is where my mind goes while I'm doing my little dance.

You're curious about tank he says after taking a sip from his tea, and for a split second I worry that Peter can read my mind. My movements are out of sync with the room, and my own body makes me self-conscious. I end up sitting down in the seat in front of him.

Tank makes people nervous.

It looks painful I say and immediately regret what I just implied. *I mean, it seems heavy.*

It's Button who is the heavy one and I'm impressed by how long she has been sleeping. Maybe it's worth putting her down in the bassinet.

My only company he explains, and his words make sense to me. *And the music.*

I ask him if he has always played the accordion and he replies since he knew what music was. But it's slowed down now. It's getting harder for him to hold and breathe and play at the same time. The tubes get entangled, fingers tire too easily, he gets frustrated.

While Peter sits in my living room, drinking tea, accompanied by the occasional silence, something is set in motion. The story of the tank is revealed.

He shares that when he first met Agata, he was a locksmith and already a smoker for over two decades. When they married, he was a photocopying technician and promised to quit smoking. He always wanted to run his own typesetting company, but technology caught up with him and passed him faster than he could teach himself how to use computers properly. It wasn't the same. Agata helped him get a job as a guard at a botanical garden, and he didn't mind all that standing around. He liked the people-watching. It was when she died this summer that his lungs caved. Even after having never touched a cigarette for years, the body implied it didn't want to go on without her. There was little reason to leave the apartment. Over forty years of marriage and music and moss, and now he has to carry this metal cylinder around. Why bother leaving the apartment? He was ready to end it.

I started hearing the baby. He says this as if it was a response to some question he was hoping to answer. I ask him if they had any children.

No children.

He doesn't give me a reason why or tell me if it was ever considered. He suggests that in a way, the plants were her children and he drinks from his cup.

What are you going to do with the plants?

Peter shrugs his shoulders. Jokes about letting them take over the apartment like some man-eating plant will conquer his place upstairs. He changes the subject out of frustration or simply old age.

Agata did this thing, after taking a bath. She would put her index finger in her ear and swish it back and forth for a while. Told him it was itchy in there but refused to use a Q-tip. It drove him crazy. And he hated that she took a bath every day. He cradles the cup of tea. When he complained to her about using too much water, she built a drainage system in their apartment. It filtered and recycled the water, even watered the plants on the fire escape.

Again he drinks.

She was too smart for him; more often than not she brimmed with hope.

While I'm listening to Peter, an interplay of sorts happens. In our continued conversation I am not sure if he is talking about Agata or if I am telling him about my mother. We both have gentle explanations of a person we hold love for, and I can't help but compare these two deaths that are shared between us.

He remembers her smell, subtle but as clear as the air in a forest.

She always had dirt under her nails.

Makeup was never a part of her routine.

She always had to sit down after going to the bathroom and it made her embarrassed. I had to keep quiet for a few minutes whenever that happened and couldn't look her in the eyes to avoid making her feel ashamed.

At the beginning of each year, she was always the first one in the water and the last one to come out by the end of the summer.

He remembers she once said that cooking was just a means to eat.

She liked to run hot water under her wrists to get warm.

He remembers her debilitating migraines. I remember she always wanted to be outside, wherever she was.

There were many days, early on in their relationship, where they slept outside under the open sky. They were still children.

He remembers never seeing her clearly, as if she were always slipping through his fingers. I remember often questioning why she loved me.

It's a slow-flowing day. Not a word in sight. But plenty of numbers: first, little ones—the seconds wrapping around in minutes and the minutes turning toward hours. The problem is that the hours have a harder time yielding to the days and weeks. I didn't expect there would be so much agony in waiting when it came to the state of being pregnant, but it's all I do.

I move my laptop to the couch in the hope that sitting somewhere else in the apartment will make me more motivated about the pages that I need to accomplish by the end of the day. Changing positions doesn't help. This day is going to disappear, taking itself with or without me having accomplished anything. I grudgingly return to my desk in the bedroom.

I turn to our window that faces another apartment building. I see that someone is using a shower curtain as blinds. Someone else is using the window to hold up their curtain—the edges of the fabric stick out in uneven ruffles. Another neighbor has kept their Christmas lights on in their windowsill. Day and night, an eternal glow emanates from their window.

As I scan the building opposite ours, I see a black cat treading down our fire escape. It holds its elegance, even on the skinny railings, and plants itself in front of our window. The sitting cat stares at me. There's no expression on its face that I can read, only observation, like what kind of a simple woman is this at her desk? What is her purpose? The cat keeps watching and pats the window with its paw. Its claws make a delicate tapping sound against the glass that's both soothing and nerve-racking. The cat meows. I don't move. The cat is now gawking, making me almost embarrassed, or at least self-aware. Well, what is my purpose? I start shuffling some notes and open dictionaries, bite on the end of a pen, stretch the spine of a book—it should seem like I'm working.

The woman from upstairs steps down the fire escape. She shows herself as quite tall and slim with a sharp angle to her haircut. Her hands have prominent veins and discolorations that are so naturally linked to old age, but the short hair gives her continued youthfulness.

She moves toward the cat and scoops up the feline with both hands. This maneuver is done with only a quick peek inside our window, perhaps she doesn't want to fully snoop. On her way back up, she holds the railing with one hand and the cat with the other. It's a motherly gesture like a furry female picking up their cub by the neck. After a few steps they are completely gone.

Once they both disappear, I can't decide who I am more jealous of: The graceful cat or the determined neighbor. Both are on the outside looking in, with someone from the inside wanting out.

I give up on work for the rest of the day and decide to go for a walk.

The walk is only moderately satisfying, some restlessness persists, and I regret not joining the company of the woman and the cat upstairs.

A nurse came into my room in the morning and said that there was a lactation consultant getting ready for a class at the end of the hall. She sounded encouraging with a caring tone in her voice. She was a wholesome-looking woman with broad shoulders and layers of mascara over and under her eyes.

Why don't I take the baby and you take your pillow—we'll stroll over there together.

Before I gave her my acceptance, she scooped up Button and placed her in a kind of baby cart. A silver cross dangled delicately from her neck as she moved around in the room. I slipped my feet into a pair of sandals and stood up. Blood rushed down to my legs and I felt faint. The room closed in on me. I leaned against the edge of the bed and tied a robe around my bulging waist as I waited for my sight to come back and the room to clear. I walked around the bed and exited my space. Each step irritated the stitches, elevated trepidation.

It's all right the nurse said. *We'll take it slow.*

She rolled Button farther away from me and the distance quickly became unbearable.

Don't forget your pillow she added.

I turned around and moved painfully along, grabbing and hugging my nursing pillow as deliberately as a small child with their beloved stuffed toy. Other women started leaving their rooms and entered the hallway at the same slow pace, also freshly injured from the war of birth. I speculated if this is what infirmaries had once resembled and joined the stream of wounded soldiers.

We shuffled our way down the hall that seemed a mile long. I thought about a sacred island that could be designated for us.

Picture a giant maternity ward on top of a mountain. That's where we should go to give birth because there we will be smothered in nurses and pillows, pampered with dimmed lights, fresh fruit, ice cream, croissants, olives, cheese, and foot rubs.

We won't be pushing; we will be releasing, giving in to gravity.

Our babies arrive and after we are cleaned up from birth our bodies are wrapped in heated blankets that smell of lavender. Someone kindly massages our necks in slow circular motions. We float in warm waters and our newly milk-filled breasts bobble gently on the surface like red buoys.

This is if things go right.

If things don't go right, we are forced to surrender to all the help and support given to us in order to survive. If the baby doesn't survive but you do, you are granted permanent residency on the island. You may pursue any unfulfilled dream on the island. Be an artist or a baker, a chemist or a welder, a sailor or a French teacher. Take that ikebana class you've always wanted to. The place is big enough for you to carve out a new life of your own choosing and small enough not to frighten you about making a change. The next steps (on the island or back on the continent) are for you to decide, whenever. Take your time.

Since shit is fucked.

I take it back, this happens if things go right.

If things go wrong and the baby arrives, the island tries to make it right.

Two or three days after birth, buggies take us down to bunga- lows that are by the shore (so no need for those noise machines). That's where we wine and dine with the babies wrapped in cotton, their lips clutched to our sensitive nipples. After eating and drinking, we sleep, we feed our babies some more, we eat some more, we lean back on pillows, we sleep on our stomachs, finally. Turn onto your back if you so wish.

We sing and hum more than we talk and listen to attention- seeking birds debate throughout the day. All day long we wear robes. They're made out of fabrics we enjoy having against our skin—linen, silk, Tencel, whatever you prefer.

We receive help with nursing or holding our babies and we step in with a set of bare breasts if one of us runs out of milk.

What comes in abundance here is patience and support. It's cheesy but true.

Some months later, when we decide to return to our homes on the continent, a helicopter will take us and our babies back. We can stay longer if we are not ready yet. After all, certain wounds heal slower than others.

The helicopter ride might sound scary, but think of it as a new chapter in your life. As you are lifted away from the island and see the contours of the wild landscape, as you hang exposed above the deep and dangerous sea, you may begin to feel a little spiritual. The island starts to morph into a large nipple or an unusual birthmark while you keep getting lifted higher and higher. Life seen from above often makes things easier to grasp than from within. So perhaps motherhood, the idea that we are made of it, doesn't become such a big fucking deal. You are it, and yet, in that noisy chopper, while you are holding your *bundle of joy,* you are also given the chance to lean out and drop it.

See the bundle fall from such great height. Watch the silent plunge into the water.

The pilot won't judge.

Once a small group of us, five or six, joins the lactation class, we each walk toward a chair that's lined up against a wall and attempt to sit down. With a pained expression on our faces and each of us holding on to the chair in one way or another, we manage. We sit down and the babies are distributed to the moms. A few check to see if their tags match their babies'. One new mom starts shaking from the sensation of sitting and her exhales come out in quick puffs. I see that her forehead has crumpled like a piece of discarded paper. She tries to apologize to the group. Her birth must have happened that morning. Button is handed to me and I'm shocked by how far removed I am from the immediate pain of birth even though it has only been one night. In sympathy of our mutual agony, I nod to the apologetic mother.

It gets better another woman whimpers across the room and we all gaze down at our babies to see if they will show us a sign of confirmation. With eyes closed, the babies do nothing.

The consultant is already in the room and has been patiently watching us take our seats. She has surrounded herself with life-sized baby dolls and different skin-colored pillows shaped like breasts that have patches of quarter-sized dark brown areolas sewn onto them.

Shall we get started? she says and puts a tit pillow against her chest.

The apartment has thrown up on itself. Folded laundry from some days ago is in piles here and there, waiting to be put away while it tries not to mingle with cotton cloths that are already moist from Button's spit-up. Bouquets from friends are growing fur at their stems, getting crisp at their petals, contributing to a murky smell. Dishes appear as soon as they disappear since I want to eat, always and forever. Cardboard boxes lean inelegantly against the wall, crowding the hallway. We have taken out the soft and fuzzy gifts, but John hasn't broken down all of the paper. I used to be fine with taking out the recycling, but I can barely look down the stairs outside our door anymore. The stoop, an old silent and stable friend, stands empty of my presence.

John is sitting at the dining table, eating with Button in his arms. A plate of the sweet-potato casserole lies in front of him. In between bites, he says that he hasn't been sleeping well. It's all the crying from Button.

I'm almost finished with my plate.

I'm going to put earplugs in tonight he tells me like a pronouncement.

John has an important meeting first thing in the morning and needs his sleep to make it through. I believe him, but what am I supposed to do? I couldn't make the same decision even if I wanted to.

Button is watching him from below, swaying her arms uncontrollably.

Fine I say.

I leave the table and move to the couch. A dust bunny scampers away by my feet. I move a few items of clothing to make room and find it difficult to decide on my emotions, but I don't fight him. I lean back with a still-swollen belly, wondering if this is how one builds a family—through imbalance? My breasts tingle, the tissues are moving, the milk is going to drop any minute. Me and my puppies are going to go through another night alone. I make the face of someone about to cry but don't give in to crying.

Once John has finished eating, he stands up with Button in the nook of one arm and the empty plate in the other. He moves over to the kitchen as if he has given up on this evening and leaves the plate in the sink. My empty plate is left on the dining table. He comes back around the room and drops off Button in my lap, sighs like the world owes him a favor.

Everything is hard, except for my dick he exclaims and leaves for the other room. Button joins me in the fortress of laundry that surrounds the couch.

At least you're still funny I tell his back, and try to get comfortable. He heads for the bathroom with a small chuckle before closing the door.

That night, John rolls into bed with a sleep mask on his forehead and a pair of earplugs in one hand like he is ready to pop them as pills. Instead he twists one blue foam piece at a time

into each ear and settles on the first sleeping position of the
night. He changes his mind, rolls over with all his gear to kiss
me, and turns back to decide on how to lie still. The bed stops
bouncing but it still wobbles in my heavy mind. I stay on my
back and stare up into the dark room. The blues and grays and
reds of the night move ever so slightly. Right above me, I see
the break in the ceiling, shifting, deepening, widening, but I
don't want to trust my eyes. I make an attempt to address the
fissure, to share these delicate cracks above us. I try to talk over
or through the two pieces of foam in his ears.

John?

What's up?

Sometimes I get these visits.

What?

I say *I get these visits.*

John rolls over to face me as he moves his mask up to his
forehead.

What are you talking about?

When you're gone, our neighbor comes to see me. The old man from
upstairs.

Why do you let him in?

His question is a fair one.

Look John continues. *Tomorrow, go outside for a minute. Sit on the*
stoop. It would be good for the both of you.

He thinks babies need air too.

I can't. She needs me all the time and as soon as I think I have the
chance to do something, she starts up again.

John adjusts his mask.

So what do you two talk about?

I don't know. Moss.

Moss?

Mostly moss and I tell him about how I'm doing.
What does moss have to do with how you are doing?
I don't know, it just helps.

I retreat behind my words and use Button as an excuse.

Well, what about joining a moms' group? John asks. It's the final question he has left in him because maybe a random old man is not the appropriate company for me at this time.

Meet some new people. Get some fresh air. John throws out these last suggestions as he slowly twists the earplugs back into his ears.

It doesn't work that way I say. *You have choices. That's why you don't understand me.*

John lets silence pass between us or he is having a hard time staying awake.

You can't do this forever, you know. He pulls his mask back down.
Let's just leave it. I need to go pump anyway.
Okay, fine.
Fine.

He rolls over.

Fine...

On the couch in the living room and all strapped up to express milk, I nod off to the rhythmic machinery of the breast pump. Drops make their way to each cup so slowly, nipples leak of desperation. In the morning I will want to check where the word "resentment" comes from, but the next day I will be too tired to remember which word I had been thinking of tonight.

There will be blood.

Words from the night nurse echo through my head as I'm waking up from a nap. It's my second day at the hospital, the day has given in to the afternoon, and my vagina feels like it just dug its own grave. From the foot of the bed, John brings me Button and I try to stay comfortable with a giant ice pack between my legs, but the classic image of the atomic bomb over Hiroshima with its mushroom head lifting above some innocent clouds charges through my mind.

I need to use the bathroom.

I turn to one side of the bed, where John is settled into his hospital chair with a laptop in his lap, but before he has even gotten moderately comfortable and able to get any work done, he replaces the computer with Button, cradling her as if she is made of eggshell, and I turn around to face the bathroom.

It's only four steps away, but I don't know if I can make it.

You'll want to pat the vagina, not wipe. Pat the vagina.

What? John says. *Are you okay?*

Squirming with discomfort, I say *Sorry. I'll be okay—just need, the bathroom.*

Embarrassment swells underneath my aching skin. I wish he didn't have to see me like this.

—

After closing the bathroom door, I take a peek at myself in the mirror. Swollen eyes stare back at me. Guess I lost that fight. I fill a small squirting tube with lukewarm water. I pull down my mesh underwear and detach a blood-soaked pad from between my legs. The red is the color of immediacy and life.

I chuck the heavy pad in a trash bin that's lined with a plastic bag, and the bag loses its grip on the bin. With the throw of the pad, it falls to the bottom. I try to pee without getting urine over my stitches. If I lean forward enough it works some, but it still stings. Legs shake a little. It's also been two days and I haven't pooped. My anus pulsates into the shape of a cauliflower. Just the thought of the energy I would have to expel in order to take a shit frightens me. Instead I grab the tube of water and squirt it up my vagina. The freshness of the water provides temporary relief.

I rip a couple of strips of toilet paper and pat my swollen lips. I can't remember the last time I saw my vagina, closer to a year than less. A duo of blood clots drop into the toilet bowl, they remind me of raw chicken liver and in the water they leave an elegant trail of red behind. This is to signal: there is no going back.

I decide to leave my underwear on the floor and strip naked, letting the hospital gown turn into a small pile around my feet. I turn on the shower and preview my bare body while waiting for the hot water to come on. I scan my breasts and belly, the linea nigra still connects my belly button to my hairy vulva. The nipples glare an animalistic brown. I don't talk to myself.

I take a careful step into the shower, moving slowly, like an assault victim who has been given permission to wash the crime off her.

The water is a blessing. I thank it as it comes pouring out of the showerhead.

Thank you thank you tthdank you dank you dnk yu u o. As if this is the first time my body experiences the sensations of water.

Ugh.

I exhale and give guttural sounds to my pathetic emotions. I bow forward and hang, and I am so heavy I almost tip over. I let the water do its thing. Dank you, again.

The sprays are warm and wet, it is all I want right now.

The steady shower stream tunes out John calling for me. The noise shushes Button's cries.

Let me stay here I say to the water. Let me stay. Grant me permission. Please.

Please.

The city outside our building sounds like an untuned orchestra trying to get its act together. John comes at me with his entire body as we are lying in bed. He wants to have sex with me tonight. I can smell what he had for lunch, and his weight overpowers more than it soothes. My body wants to recoil, it is hypersensitive to his touch, to air, to residues and smells; I am something extraterrestrial. I can notice the temperature shift in the room. I can sense the nausea in my throat, the fur on my tongue, the linings of the protective vessel I am becoming.

I'm pregnant I blurt out.

John stops his worming.

Really?

I wanted it to be your Christmas present, but I feel awful. And I'm pregnant.

My arms stretch out in front of him to get some space.

Holy shit he laugh-cries, and hugs me.

John's neck smells of remnants from the day. I'm scared I'll throw up on him.

That was fast he says. It wasn't really, but it's fine.

John untangles himself from our embrace and we spend the rest of the evening talking about what kind of parents we desire to be, filling in each other's gaps of expectations, promises, wishes, sharing the ways in which we will be different than others or imitate the best parts of our parents. Ultimately remaining clueless to what next year will entail and unaware that from now on, time will be the main character and culprit in our lives.

Once it's okay to wet the baby—I think they said "Give it a few days" at the hospital—John bathes Button in the kitchen. Like some godless ceremony, it begins with me undressing her on the changing table in the nursery. I take my opened package and pass her on as he stands ready and shirtless to accept Button by the sink. John has placed a small tub under the faucet and inside it he has a smaller plastic insert that's shaped like a slide. A clean unfolded towel awaits next to him. With both hands he takes Button from me and places her on the insert. It's almost as if she is sitting up. Each hand of hers makes a fist. Her arms close in, her legs cross at the ankles. Her legs are as long as her torso.

The kitchen shows the remains from the day; onion peels are scattered around the cutting board, a knife with the juice of a wet vegetable shines on the counter.

Don't you want to move the knife out of the way? I ask John, but he is too focused on making sure Button doesn't slide away.

John turns on the faucet like he is going to do the dishes, but this time he checks the temperature of the water with the inside of his wrist before lightly pressing the button that will spray her down. Water gently hits Button's small body and she makes faces that are filled with equal amounts of fear and intrigue.

Even though the size of our apartment doesn't grant me the chance to go very far, I leave them to be alone. I lie down in the bedroom, look up at the ceiling, and can't help but wonder what Peter is doing all by himself upstairs. Meanwhile, John is describing what he is doing.

First we wash the little facey and then we wash the necky.

He is running through all of the major body parts. I close my eyes and can't help but listen. John never says *vulva* or *vagina*, but I know when he is washing her between her legs because he goes quiet for an extra second.

Suddenly he is washing her *cheekies*. First one butt cheek and then the other.

I open my eyes and meet the ceiling again, staring back at me. How immediately we sexualize.

It must be that the decision not to name a body part is what creates a tension against the rest of the body.

When I change her diaper, I do the opposite in Swedish.

I am wiping your vulva, which came from *volva,* "womb," "bulb of the vestibule." *Does Volvo have anything to do with "volva"?*

I turn to Button for the answer. Probably more obvious with *volvere,* "to roll," although I wouldn't be surprised if it was linked.

Once I'm done with the explaining and in the process of giving her a new diaper, I check to make sure Button's anus and vulva look all right.

By all right I mean intact. Although I'm not sure what I'm expecting to see. Nobody has access to her body except for John and me, and yet I check every single time, mesmerized by the sight of her miniature sex that is empty of all associations, or as if I am suspicious.

I mean, I love John, but what if one day he slips a finger inside her vagina when he is changing her diaper? He would never do this, but what if he would? To violate a body, the dance only takes one forward motion. At every point of us touching her we are so close to the intimate pieces of what we view to be the most sacred part of a girl. Button is completely oblivious to the laws around her body. For how long can I keep it that way? When does the outside world step in? And what is holding John back? Is his decency a façade? What if he is deceiving me? What if he impregnated me to molest my child?

Miffo is lurking.

John can't be the predator in this scenario. I can't allow my mind to turn on him. I am the guilty one.

The ceiling doesn't reply as if I just now spoke to it. Only signals the expanded fracture in one corner. I fix my eyes on it to see if I can catch its slight movement. My eyes spasm.

After a few minutes, I can't lie down anymore.

I get up and watch from the doorway how John turns Button over to wash her back. She is as long as his forearm, and he holds her with one arm while he sprays water with the other. Her skin shines, it's so smooth, slippery, resembling a wet chicken fillet after it's been rinsed. From the counter, the knife twinkles at me, wanting to be held.

John handles her quickly so as not to lose his grip. I'm standing by, praying. If he dropped her, how swiftly would my relief come? Could I be sure of its arrival?

Button is so fully unformed. Un-fully formed, yet she has all of the parts that we are familiar with. I watch my mind take over what I see. In the corner of my eye, the knife glimmers, as if it's moving. If it were in my hand, what would I be capable of? What would I do if I saw all of her parts chopped up on the table?

A grotesque image appears and I have to shake it off straightaway.

Motherhood might be about having lost my mind, and I am about to spend the rest of my life searching for it.

The duo in the kitchen grabs my attention again.

John gives Button a final rinse. He places her on the flat towel next to the sink and wraps her up like a burrito. This is when he begins to coo, calling her *my little bun,* and the hunger takes over my thinking. Button squirms awkwardly under the towel, unaccustomed to her head being dried. John brings his wrapped bundle back to her room, and from the doorway I can see that he unfolds the towel, one corner at a time. Button squeals. John agrees with what she is saying as he puts tiny items of clothing on her and gently pulls at the seams.

While they are having this conversation, I should get ready for the night. I turn to the kitchen and want something in the fridge to speak to me, may it satisfy this forever hunger. In the open compartments, I also search for my mind, because these perverted thoughts are starting to scare me. If only it were so easily found in the vegetable drawer, hiding behind a box of unrinsed cremini mushrooms.

I grab a red pepper and eat it like an apple. I swallow without much chewing. The tissues under my breast begin to tickle, they know it's time soon. But first I eat and drink and drink and eat like there is no tomorrow and it's funny how that saying goes because my tomorrow was today and my today is already my tomorrow. I eat some more and then some, leaving drawers empty except for the dry skin of onions.

Okay, she's ready! John exclaims proudly from the nursery.

I swallow and swallow and swallow, and wipe my mouth with the sleeve of the robe.

Let the night begin.

Google:

postpartum symptoms
postpartum anxiety definition
postpartum anxiety symptoms
postpartum treatment
sexual abuse infant
how to tell if your baby has been sexually abused

How's the pain level? the doctor in green scrubs asks.

I don't know how to describe it.

He gives me an arbitrary scale to work with because I can't accept that his one-to-five is the same one-to-five in my native tongue of pain.

Are you hemorrhaging? he asks another time he comes in to check on me.

Some. I haven't had a bowel movement in about two days.

Not hemorrhoids. I mean, are you experiencing excessive bleeding? Is blood coming down your legs? He indicates how it can gush by running a hand down his leg.

Oh. No—I don't think so.

My tits are out when he enters the room one last time; this time to tell me that everything is clear. The curtains are pulled to the side.

You're good to go he says like a flight attendant checking me in at the counter, and he lets me know we should be out by eleven a.m. If only I were at a nice hotel, I would call the front desk and delay my checkout.

How about six months from now.

Excuse me? the doctor interrupts, and I wave my words away with a heavy head.

We're having this non-conversation as Button is trying to figure out the left nipple. As we all can see, it is right in front of her. I suppose I need to trust the doctor that I'm able enough to head home.

John arrives with the car seat. He carries it like he has never carried one before, which explains his clunky movements. The men in the room make small nods of acknowledgment to each other. My tits are still out, making indirect eye contact.

The doctor is writing his initials all over my chart. Without taking his eyes off the pad, he says that nurses will check me out.

Do you have any questions? he asks with a chest already facing the exit. He doesn't even want to look at my bare breasts or look me in the eyes. I can't be that saggy.

I'm not sure.

I fiddle with getting Button to see the nipple. It's. Right. There. In. Your. Face. Baby. My own face begins to flush, my nipples get a beating.

Well then he says. The man exits the room one last time and never comes back.

John, on the other hand, is staring at my chest, curious about the mechanics of latching on the baby. He comes closer and makes affectionate and reassuring sounds toward Button. Finally, she gets it and drinks. I lean back, let my head sink into the pillows. Is there a way to unbutton her from me?

The morning parade of hospital staff members begins while I'm still in bed.

John leaves to get a cab for us. A cleaning woman I've never seen before enters the room and gives me a gift bag filled with two bath toys shaped like ducklings and a tiny orange froth towel. It moves me beyond my saggy core, and I thank her with all my might before she disappears. The day nurse bounces into my room, swoops Button up, and starts rearranging things. She puts Button down in the clear bassinet. She undresses me from the waist down, changes my underwear, gives a quick inspection, cracks an ice pack that she wedges between my legs with a new clean pad, and hikes up a fresh pair of mesh undies. She is a professional and I inhale from the chill of the ice pack.

It's looking good down there the nurse says and starts moving around the bed, pushing buttons, checking off papers, changing medical items from here to there. She hands me a large folder with all the necessary paperwork and provides a dizzying amount of additional information about how to care for the baby.

She explains that I need to start pumping milk straightaway, and it's best to store it for the time being. My milk will come in properly by the middle of the week, that's also around the same time when we should take the baby for her first checkup. I'm listening but not taking much in.

I should get dressed, but the thought of my own clothes on my skin feels utterly foreign, it's actually a kind of metal armor I've never worn before but now have to find the strength to carry. I turn toward the ceiling. There's nothing distinct about the room to make me remember it, which also pains me since great feats were accomplished here not too long ago. The body made it through, ultimately.

I'm looking good "down there," she said. Sounds like the destination you reach after a transatlantic flight, but it still makes me want to embrace her.

I'm going to leave you to it. Don't forget to take everything. The nurse has already moved on from us.

Uninterested in my gratitude or what I'm going to do with the rest of my days, she leaves my life as quickly as she entered it.

Do we really need three thermometers?

A few minutes later, John is back from the outside world. He thinks I'm crazy for emptying the drawers.

They can't use these again anyway.

It saddens me to think that I will bleed through three twelve-packs of maternity pads, but something about how the nurse spoke makes me abide by her every word. Her tone was so bland but direct and intentional. She understood my immediate future.

In a hospital pack that is given to all new moms lies a pamphlet that asks bluntly in purple font: "Do you wish to harm your child?" I suppose there is wishing and there is wishing. There is also "desire," "need," "urge," combined with *gärna,* willingly.

As I'm stuffing pads and packs and packets of everything related to the baby and me into tote bags, I keep wanting to talk to the night nurse, the one whose name I remember.

I poke my head out of the room and ask for her. After a swift elimination method to understand which night nurse I mean, her colleagues tell me she's not here but they will pass on my good wishes. The ladies float away into different spaces, down longer hallways. There's nobody left to cling to at the maternity ward. I pull my head back into my room. I'm starting to understand that I'm going to be left completely alone to care for Button.

John dresses Button in an outfit that makes her look unreal, doll-like, but still something that can die any minute. She is a baby chick that accidentally left its nest too soon. I'm kind of standing around in between moments and movements that don't grant me any direction.

Another new person arrives to wheelchair me out because I'm not allowed to carry Button, and it's not until I sit down that I think it must be because they don't want my stitches to come undone. John carries the baby in the car seat. Wobbling forward, he might fall over any minute.

The doors to the elevator haven't even closed and I want to go back to the time before I gave birth. Any new step, any new set of walls, reverberates within. I'd like to return to my hospital bed, please. Who can I speak to for permission? The rolling continues into the elevator.

Once we hit the entry level, I'm allowed out of the wheelchair. Before I get to turn around by the exit, I see two broad-shouldered men and one skinny old guard who are idling around the reception area. They walk toward us as we are exiting. Apparently our new unit of three needs to pass some security control before we leave. Almost in unison, the men tell me to put my arm out, the one with the tag on it. I am required to read off the seven-digit number on Button's tiny ankle.

It's for your security, ma'am. You wouldn't want to leave with the wrong baby, now would you.

I give the man a glassy look.

What if the baby left with the wrong mother? I ask.

Excuse me?

She's joking John clarifies.

The men turn to me.

Ma'am, the seven digits, please.

They talk like they know what's at stake. It doesn't seem as though the task requires three adult men to perform, but I give them what they ask for.

7481350.

The skinny one silently reads the tag on my arm. Granting us permission, he says *All good to go.*

Congratulations, ma'am says the other, right on time. The third one chimes in, and they all clear the way. John smiles widely, as content as a Labrador, perhaps also with some relief.

When we exit the building we are met with the insistent August sun and people who are using their day as if it's the weekend. Doors, cars, birds, people, air, it all sounds louder to me. Through tiny vibrations I can even sense the traffic noise between my legs. When the sunlight hits my face, I simultaneously welcome and despise the feeling. Even without the front weight, I wobble down the street. Strangers walking by congratulate me and smile at a sleeping baby in a car seat, meanwhile I am frightened.

I can't believe I did this to myself.

You okay? John asks but is not interested in an answer as he excitedly waves to our driver, who is slowly rolling up to the entrance of the hospital. Many doors of a black car open.

I let John and the driver move and maneuver things around me. For half a minute they make all the decisions, positioning where our bags and everyone else should go. I stand motionless, observing. They click Button in and I climb awkwardly into the car to situate myself in the back seat. I can still see her in the row in front of me, but I can't help but think that my arm has been chopped off and she is the phantom pain that dangles heavily from my shoulder.

Don't worry John assures me shortly thereafter. *She's all buckled in.*

The ride home is bumpy and long. I hold on to the handle above my head, sometimes with both hands.

When we arrive at our apartment building, I have the tote bags from the hospital but I don't know where my keys are or who has any of my personal belongings. It's as if I've been robbed and didn't immediately notice but *It's okay,* John reassures again, while carrying car-seated Button. He lets us into the building. That's when fatigue hits me.

I walk up our three flights of stairs, holding on to the walls, scared of falling backward, worried I'll rip something. At my most sensitive point, my legs shake slightly.

Looks like these books arrived for you John says, kicking a couple of boxes out of the way to get to our door. The traces of my former self are unrecognizable and strange.

Once home and inside, with the door unlocked and the three of us past the hallway, John takes charge of placing all of our things down and away from us. I close the door. He leans the tote bags against the wall and they slide down to the floor. I stand watching as he goes to unsnap Button from the car seat.

Welcome home, baby girl.

He lifts her high with a gesture that resembles a sacred act observed at a church service. It is obvious that John is pleased. In this moment, I am not sure if I am happy for him.

Once the apartment has accepted Button or she has blessed our place by her presence, John grabs a pair of scissors from the top kitchen drawer. He comes over to snip the hospital tags off my arm and off Button's foot. I let him hold my wrist and then watch how the scissors graze the thin layer of her skin before he cuts her tag.

Freedom he exhales, and smiles.

I can't stop thinking about you. I walk around in the streets with my secret about you. I meet the occasional friend for a coffee but drink tea and don't mention that you are the one thing that is on my mind. I don't even mind that I'm not drinking coffee right now. I edit at my desk with a hand on my belly, although it is ridiculously early to be showing even a bump. I welcome John more affectionately when he comes home from work. The possibility of you is constantly on my mind. But I realize there is nothing exciting about describing the unknown or the potential. Conjuring up your existence is of no value to anyone else but me. How strange that this power is neglected in women, because it is witchcraft.

If I think too closely about it, maybe today brought on too much simple pleasure, and that makes me anxious. The sun was bright, the air crisp, full of potential and bird chatter. I worked and wrote and walked and drank tea and worked some more and there wasn't much more to ask for.

In the middle of the day, John texted

Mwah.

Surely, this kind of goodness will be snapped up and taken away from me any minute. Because you know I hate surprises.

Puss puss I echoed in Swedish. Kiss kiss.

—

That evening when I shower before going to bed, I run the soap around the sides of my thighs and can't help but worry. I circle the whitish liquid up and around and under my armpits, half-heartedly hugging myself. I fondle my wet breasts and wonder if there are cancer cells lurking underneath the tissue of my skin. I think about dying and how I would prefer not to die. The stakes are suddenly much higher with you in the picture. I want you and I want to be alive, loving you. This is the purest gesture I can give you.

Before I became a translator you should know that I toyed with the idea of becoming a filmmaker or an archivist. I dreamed of different scenarios: checking people's tickets on the train as we rolled from one city to another or managing the front desk at an elderly home and taking down visitors' signatures. I imagined myself as anyone. I understand you may not find that ambitious enough.

My problem has always been that I wanted to be German, Polish, or Italian as much as I envisioned myself as a Japanese woman living and working in a rural town near some form of running water. Each vastly different life was attractive, and most were tragically unobtainable. It had to do with money, the lack of it, but also that I lost my mother at a young age. It's only now that I can admit it does something to you, shifts the lenses, defines your idea of "tragedy." Makes you hate surprises.

Maybe I should have been a spy, but I ended up amounting to little. It's a shame you can't make a living by simply observing people. Whenever I held office jobs, I was always

more intrigued with the person who came to fix the printer or
the cleaning woman who rolled her cart down the long corridor than anyone else on the rest of the floor. I wanted to hear
their stories. It became clear to me that I wanted to be the bar-
tender as much as I wanted to be the drinker. Eventually, I
translated the notion of knowing little about many things into
literature. And the beauty of the job is that anyone can become
a translator.

Before I fall asleep, I make a grand proclamation: Motherhood
will give me purpose.
  Purpose, purpos, porpos, porposer, poser, pausare, pausa, please.

The next day, I sit and translate and eat crackers and cheese
and I could do this forever. I look up words I don't know, try to
understand how they should be used, but end up bending them
to my liking. Crumbs fall into the cracks of the novel I'm working on and my greasy fingers smudge the pages. The suicide in
the book is imminent.
  I crave pain au chocolat. I'd love...almonds. Vanilla ice
cream. I chew a round apple skinny. I daydream about a painful foot rub with heated stones under my soles.
  I snack my way through the first draft, the first trimester,
and nap my way along the other two.
  Sometimes when John comes home he honeys me and
inquires *What's with the trail of apple cores?*

There's knocking on the door.

From the bedroom I hear John opening the door to friends who have been waiting an extra beat to come in. Before I go out to the hallway to greet them, I adjust my hair, check for milk stains on my shirt, and inhale to prepare. I'm already tired before I have started talking and regret that I haven't washed my face.

My immediate participation in welcoming our visitors is as if I'm listening in on other people's conversations taking place right in front of me. I am a numbing agent.

Shoes are taken off and placed outside the door. There's awkward leaning against the wall. Hands are washed immediately after entering. Gifts are kindly given. I place what is handed to me on the kitchen counter, the only stable thing in this apartment. I see John quickly bending down under the sink to grab a bottle of hand sanitizer. He places it on the counter.

Friends come to hold the baby and treat Button as a kind of sacred and blessed statue. They smell her head, hoping she will give them good luck for the future. I'm meant to hand her over.

Friends tell me she is so *Aww* this and so *Oh* that, until she spits up on their sleeve. Her reflex is so innocent, but nobody is keen to clean up.

Here you go they say.

My reflex is to apologize, I must have read somewhere that that's what new mothers do, and I jump to wet a corner of a kitchen towel before returning to take the unwanted baby.

I'm very sorry. Again with the apologies.

Friends are curious to know how she sleeps, fluffing me with questions like we are observing the weather.

Friends assure me they will want to participate in the child's life and grab Button back from me while I'm wiping settled milk from their sleeves.

Friends stare into Button's closed eyes, waiting for a sign. Friends return her once Button relieves herself. I finally understand the speed of "skedaddle."

These friends are from John's childhood. Friends since five years ago or last year, friends from different circles, all mostly from John's world again, but some also from publishing.

Some of them acknowledge how *sad* it is that my mother is not here to hold the baby like they are holding the baby. Some wonder how I'll possibly manage when John returns to work but don't offer to come visit during the week. A number of them leave a container of food and say *Don't worry about the Tupperware.* But some friends won't reach out again until there's a birthday, and I don't know this yet. Some other friends will never return, again without my knowledge. A wall is erected— the one that separates the child-ed with the child-less. It is built brick by brick from the mutual understanding that we do not understand each other anymore. So it goes. When will I know?

One friend texts that she has to come and see the baby. She insists in all caps and exclamation points, then cancels twice.

Another friend shows up and says *Everything seems to be in order.* No one asks about me or my work, or what thoughts flicker through my mind all day long, alone with a baby.

—

We are endless loops of repetition.

John is elated by the steady stream of visitors. After all, they know him better than they know me. While I'm holding Button, he grabs their jackets and flowers, motions to the bathroom with full hands while he throws clothes or tote bags onto our bed and hands me a bouquet that needs a vase. He doesn't stop talking, but before he tells and retells Button's birth, I interject with

Sorry, would you mind? and glare at friends' shoes after they've washed their hands. They don't mind at all, they say, and step outside before reentering with socks they didn't expect to show off. As they're apologizing for their poor decision in foot covering, I briefly consider asking them to wash their hands again.

There's also hand sanitizer over here.

My body holding Button with the bouquet points to the kitchen counter. Lots of body pointing in this household today. They should get the hint. But why should I be the one willing to let her go?

John continues the birth story from wherever he left off. The story gets juicier with each new guest. I lay the flowers down next to the untouched hand sanitizer.

I spend little time talking to our visitors since it is also impossible to maintain or even pay attention to conversations when my chest is constantly producing milk. I can't help but think of *alstra*, or *generera*, or *producera*, from Latin *producer:* "lead or bring forth, draw out"—from *pro*, "before," plus *ducere*, "to bring." Please bring me the time that came before this.

A distraction is constantly churning in the background, spinning and spinning, and then it seeps out when I am full in the form of milk. So what am I supposed to say? There is nothing interesting about caring for a baby, nothing being created here.

Interesting—"engaging the attention, so as to excite interest"—tell me that "it is of importance, to make a difference" to make a "legal claim of right"—creating *ett alster*, a work, a thing, a birthing, but anyway, futile digressions that please no one else but me...

While John is entertaining our guests, I let myself be an outsider and imagine my upstairs neighbor playing the accordion for my amusement again. The tunes of the clunky instrument come streaming wide and sound deep but are muffled through the ceiling. I've decided only I can hear it.

From under the pile of jackets on the bed, the large maternal spider emerges with an abdomen that expands once she has fully materialized. She walks up to me with elegance and some determination. I don't hear or see anyone else in the crowded apartment. One of her prickly legs takes my hand. With the other, I give her Button and she slides down into a webbed backpack that the eight-legged creature carries without a care in the world. Button rests on her thorax and we can now hold hands. She begins leading me around and around in the living room, following the blue songs coming from above.

From the fire escape and through the window, we can be seen twirling, swaying—she gives me sweet liberation as I stare deeply into one pair of her four pairs of eyes, it's dizzying, she's dazzling, I am alive again—but really, who are we kidding here, instead

I sit, I am sitting, sweating from nursing and almost falling asleep from listening. The end. The end of me. There's no maternal waltz, no accordion exhaling or inhaling from above.

In the entryway to our building hangs a board made of cork on the wall. On the board there are a small number of announcements and important contact information for the management team in case of emergencies. Under the board is a radiator that is always hotter than necessary at any given moment of the year.

Today there is a new notice on the board, a note of a memorial service for our upstairs neighbor with the Eastern European–sounding last name. The woman is survived by her husband, but no kids, siblings, or parents are mentioned in the photocopied obituary. Her most recent publication on moss and urban environmental pollution is listed. As I'm reading the note, I have a hand on my large belly to comfort myself.

I didn't know there was such a thing as bryology I tell John later that night over dinner after I mention the sudden death of our upstairs neighbor.

It's weird that we never saw her he says.

Or sad.

Or sad we conclude.

We debate over whether or not we should go to the memorial service. I find it strange to show up for someone dead when we didn't even know the extent to which they were alive. John thinks it would be a kind gesture. Somehow we end up bickering about it, both unsure of why it becomes such a big deal.

Can every life choice while being pregnant be blamed on hormones? John seems to think so and says that I shouldn't be able to get out of this so easily. I beg to differ. More out of stubbornness than any kind of argument that makes sense. We go to bed that night facing away from each other but seem to make up silently in our sleep as we don't even mention the fight the next day. From inside the belly, the baby makes sweeping motions, keeping me awake and uncomfortable most nights.

By not reaching a decision about the memorial service we end up not going. A week later the notice has fallen to the floor. The paper is a bit crinkled, with a stain added from a footprint or a stroller. Either way, it's gone the day after, leaving me tempted to speculate about the fate of the black cat upstairs.

I'm having revelations about my stupidity. I suddenly don't know . . . well, *things*. Maybe it is not so suddenly and it can be blamed on Button's arrival, but these days, if I have a think about it, I don't really know how touch screens work or how to explain electricity in a basic way. Airplanes impress me, batteries are cool, toilets also. That there's clean water coming out of our taps each day is astonishing. As for history, I can't remember the years in which the Cold War took place. Not that it's necessarily required of me to remember, but the past really doesn't stick right now. As for the present: Is Aleppo even a thing anymore? What's even going on at the Greek and Turkish borders? I wouldn't be able to share the latest about the Ebola outbreak; I have no idea if people still care about Zika or if they have moved on. And what *are* the differences between "government" and "parliament"?

I used to know the colors of most European flags, but now even borders have blurred. I believe the Scots want to break free and I have a vague understanding of the Brits being in a pickle, but that's about it.

Sometimes John reads the headlines from online newspapers to me—they often verge on the absurd, and most insinuate that we should expect the arrival of dread. I don't know if it matters much, as I am already entrenched in my state. It doesn't even give me the chance to worry about Button's future.

I also wouldn't be able to say what water is made of. I mean, what is the word, for that thing, that describes the components of water or copper or silver? The matrix of what everything contains, the chemistry of things.

Well, this Miffo has no clue.

Sleep deprivation strips from me any possibility of reattaching myself to the outside world.

What are you saying? John wonders, but shame pokes its head out and I can't rationalize it.

Never mind.

And John falls asleep.

In the lonely evening light, I look around our apartment and see cloth wipes drooping from the sides of our couch. I see hung laundry that's been picked at, empty cardboard boxes stacked inside one another. I see the immediate and absolute present. I recognize its composition and observe it without hesitation. I have been here before.

I thought I knew some things about the world, but in this new, turned-inside-out existence, I am unsure of it all. And if I don't have my words, what is left of me? Am I purely a motherless wife chained to my own mothering? Why would anyone even call this repetition mothering?

I can't help but wonder if Button took something with her when she was born. She drove me to my undoing.

I must be a *Miffo,* a freak, a delay, a hindrance, and a failure. A concept of unrest.

As if I can collect all of me in this muddle, I attempt to tell myself

Pull it together.

But pity takes over, grabs me by the arm, and reminds me that I am a monstrosity.

I take us to nurse in the next room. There's a little light coming in from the crack of the door, otherwise we are sitting in the dark. Button is a squirmy warm cocoon in my arms, drifting in and out of sleep. I am drifting in and out of sleep with her. Losing words with each blink of my heavy eyes.

Like a carousel slide projector, memories of mostly soft recollections appear in front of me. They include the person I once was with the actions I could make before Button arrived.

I am in Paris, resting my drunken head on a friend's windowsill. I am sleeping on a beach in Croatia and mosquitoes are pricking me awake. I am paging through books at an *antikvariat* and consider walking out with one under my shirt. I am waiting for a train to arrive at an empty platform in Toledo. I am lying on the ground at a museum, staring up at a large light installation. I am walking on the side of a highway. I am recording my heartbeat on Teshima Island. I am playing in the mud, in a pair of red-and-blue overalls. I am collecting rocks along a shore. I am filming my mother climbing a tree. I am eating strawberries she has grown. I am hiding cigarettes in a small wooden box. I am cutting out pictures from magazines. I am asleep at the terminal gate. I am buying a green coat on sale while rain is pouring down outside the store. I am sleeping at a friend of a friend's place on an unusually thick mattress with only one pillow and no cover. I am being driven through

North London and a boyfriend tells me this singer we both like just died. *Stabbed himself in the stomach. Can you believe it?* My boyfriend is drunk while he is driving us through the sparkling city. I am thinking of this one line from a novel that I read when I was in high school. I am in line at a pharmacy, it's two a.m. I am developing film. I am letting John take my hand in a sculpture park. I am listening to a busker while the escalator moves me farther away from him. I am walking out of a movie theater, following the stream of people onto the street as the sun is setting behind us. I am drinking an energy drink in the English section of the main library at university. It's almost nine p.m., and I need to get a few more hours of studying done. I am listening to a talk about the concept of melancholia. I am at a nightclub, alone in a dark corner, watching purple and green lasers hit people's heads on the dance floor. I am cycling past a field of rapeseed and each one is in full bloom. Sometimes I let go of the handlebars. I am picking confetti out of a friend's hair at my own wedding. I am petting a mutt on a street without a sign. I hear people walking on cobblestones. I am walking home alone at night. I am watching an ant crawl on my bare knee. I am ordering a cup of coffee. I am blowing out a candle at a restaurant. I am eating a napoleon at a pastry shop. I am walking down a dusty street in Budapest at peak summer and see the sunlight reflect from a window display. I am holding John's hand at the supermarket. I am holding John's hand at Homeland Security. I am laughing during a dinner party, throwing my head back.

Button lets out a gurgling sound and I'm back in the room with her. The line between where I was and where I am now is ever so faint. I don't know what to do with her. When can you put the baby down? Will the baby be less attached to me if I put it down? Or will the baby be more attached to me if I put it down?

I am sitting here and breathing and sitting and not even waiting but watching the memories come in and the memories come out, like waves on a shore. Waves on a shore.

I go find my phone.

Let the fluorescent light shine on my face.

Google:

what is water
what is the chemical compound for epsom salt
what is postpartum ocd
postpartum ocd symptoms

As a form of distraction from my nightly reality, I check my email, and the editor who will publish my latest translation about the woman who leads her husband to suicide wants to offer me another project: a quartet written by one of Sweden's most respected but easily overlooked contemporary female writers. The books are bestsellers in Scandinavia, and it's the first time an entire series has won the Nordic Council Literature Prize, to the fury of some. It's one of those highly ambitious projects, epic in scope, spanning generations and countries, a real milestone in her long and otherwise mostly subtle career. Without a doubt, these will be a part of *the future canon,* the editor writes in her email, and she is proud to have acquired the books.

She wants to know if I want the job. Each book is over six hundred pages long, written in the author's emblematic dense style, and the editor will give me over a year to finish each one. This would mean a handful of solid years at my desk.

According to the editor, the author insists on the same translator for the entire quartet, so they are asking for a commitment up front. She will pay royalties. She will put my name on the cover.

It is also easy on the editor because she won't need to keep finding a new translator with each publication or mess too much with scheduling. And she trusts me, doesn't need a sample translation before committing. At the end of the email, she encourages me to start reading the first volume, convinced that I'll immediately get excited about the project. She attached the pdf of the first book.

This is the most security I have ever been presented with when it comes to my work. Equal amounts of elation and fear emerge. Even if I would get bored or frustrated halfway through, it's difficult to resist.

I'm tempted to tell John about the good news, but it is past his bedtime and I don't want to ruin his sleep, we are already getting so little of it. There goes something above my head. The crack is shifting again, buckling and swelling. This time the movement is almost audible, and there are even discolorations moving into yellow tones, turning away from the original white, almost looking a bit damp. I can imagine Peter upstairs, pulling his loyal tank along the room from one end to the other.

I see that the world will go on without me, whether or not I want it to. The desk is calling. The sound is on one of those wavelengths only dogs can hear, or sleep-deprived mothers.

The desk calls.

We're in bed with our bodies in a bind. John is breathing deeply; he is on the cusp of sleep. He is not interested in talking any-more, whereas I'm unsettled and restless. These days, giving in to sleep makes me anxious. It's easy to overthink things, to get caught on words. When it comes to work, there's a place I'm trying to translate but it's so distinct to the Swedish islands that I will probably leave it as is. It may seem like the easy way out, but exoticizing the translation could be my best bet. The reader may find that approach rewarding. The next day, I'll see if I can try again.

I take John's hand and put it on my belly, which is expanding, growing, taking over, and the idea of you in it is all-consuming. It's the wonder and the unknown that I'm sleeping with.

I can't believe my mother is not here.

I know, sweetie. He coos.

John gives me one last squeeze before he falls asleep and he sleeps so instantly. His body releases willfully and easily to slumber.

The thought of my mother is held until I am repeating the same four memories that I tend to see her in: over the kitchen sink, digging her hands into wet dirt, lying on a sun chair, or riding her bicycle. Sometimes I watch her with me, observ-

ing my own recollection of a memory. Never do I allow someone else to infiltrate these moments. I do embellish the details,
make her more beautiful and kinder than she ever was in reality. I give her painted nails and a prestigious occupation, when
she was actually an ordinary person. But what else do I have at
my disposal now that she is gone.

Did the sun always follow her wherever she went? Did the
sun manage to infiltrate my memories by only appearing when
times were good? There is often sunlight when I think about
my mother.

And when I am at my happiest, I am riding behind her
observing her plain bare ankles. Wherever we went, she always
packed lightly, she must have known nothing bad would happen to us on this path that we cycled on. It was often a long
and winding road, stretching out into wide-open fields, crops,
landscapes. My mother never prepared for the worst. Maybe
that made her happier than most. Maybe her death was sweeter
because of her naivety. Maybe I should have tried to get to
know her better. Maybe then I would have been left with more
than my romanticism of her.

As my head rests on the pillow, tears fill my eye sockets.
Eventually they drip over the soft edge of my face and I join
John in sleep.

In the meantime, you continue to be a beating muscle. You
are groups and groups of cells multiplying, expanding, shape-
shifting, turning around, and stretching. Growing nails, eye-
lashes, a personality.

You are possibilities.

John and I are lying in bed next to each other. For privacy, we have put Button in her container right outside the bedroom. Just until we figure out what we are trying to do.

John is fingering me and I am kissing him. Both of these motions are slow, we are walking in the dark, feeling our way forward with whatever sliver of light reflects off our surroundings. My stitches have dissolved, freakishly they are now a part of me, and the bulge on my belly is less protrusive, but I still haven't explored the current circumstances between my legs. I view my vagina as a separate entity from me. Basically, I don't think of it, can't control it, and yet I am aware it exists somewhere, almost as some de jure sovereign state.

I put my hand on John's briefs and can tell that his hardened penis lies steadily underneath the fabric. I am jealous of how easy it all is for him, how quickly excitement happens and reveals itself, but I don't say anything to run the risk of ruining the mood. I am, however, not in the mood. There is nothing to feel, so I go somewhere else and imagine taking myself out for dinner, eating a bowl of cheesy pasta in front of candlelight, being utterly content. I have a glass of house red in my hand and there are other plates in front of me that I eat randomly but excitedly from: broccoli rabe, veal schnitzel, crusty bread, salty butter...John, on the other hand, is still searching. At some point, he must sense that I am bone dry. We are both trying to be tender. We are both trying and we are both lying. He stops kissing me and whispers

I can catch a tumbleweed in here.

Always the funny one between the two of us.

Whoosh he says, pretending to be the desert.

Very funny I say and push him away but still keep him close. After all, who am I to disagree that it is like a forgotten cave down there.

It does become uncomfortable to try to get me wet so we stop trying and continue kissing for a little while. His hard-on in my hand shrinks. The moment is over. We both know the moment is over. We are two tired and limp bodies still facing each other. We both admit the truth.

Can I go take a bath? I ask.

Sure he says and rolls away from me.

In the hot bathtub, I think about Peter's wife, Agata, and how much time she spent willingly on her knees. How she was most often in the woods, staring at the smallest specimens right in front of her feet. How she didn't need much and how the world didn't ask anything of her. How she is missed by only one person in the world. How even the moss can't feel her absence.

I think of all the many brilliant things she must have known about life, a life dedicated to searching and understanding.

I fantasize about Peter sitting next to me on the edge of the tub. He is playing pop songs on the accordion but they are slowed down, as if they have gone through the agony of war. I hum to them softly and give in to the nice acoustics of the bathroom. The oxygen tank next to me is part of the audience of two. I miss both of them dearly, comfort myself with the idea that at least I got to know Peter, the tank (and the idea of Agata) for a brief moment, and as I soak in the water, I decide to add value to that brief, fleeting time that we had. This is my baptism.

I sing

> *Di cra num sco par ium*
> *Di cra num mon ta num*
> *Di cra num ful vum*
> *Di cra num*
> *ful vum*

Later and newly awakened from a nap, I find Button sleeping on my chest. Her body, as heavy as a sack of flour, weighs on me but it's not unpleasant. A still and steady breath arises, rises and subsides from her small form that asks nothing from me in this moment. This breath provides warmth and adds to the definition of *trygghet,* comfort.

Jag känner mig trygg med dig. I whisper that I feel safe with her.

Button sleeps for longer stretches now. I continue to pump, but having given her a bottle means that John can take her without me needing to be near and I can sleep or sit at my desk, read a page in a book or search for a word that doesn't automatically come to mind. Most words still haven't fully returned but I try, it's all right, and I can brush my hair or floss. I can start translating something new, like the first part of the quartet, or I can drink a freshly brewed cup of coffee on our stoop. Choices begin to return.

I don't do this very often, but I meet a friend who has recently had a baby. We sit down for lunch at a place that serves over-priced coffee and pricey open-faced sandwiches. *But it's so tasty,* she promises, and I scoot the backless seat away from our table, trying to get comfortable and leaving space for the belly.

My belly keeps swelling, and I'm letting it speak for itself because I want to focus on eating and not talking about myself but I can only afford their soup of the day. My friend orders a lunch combo and asks me about work, assumes it'll be nice to control my free time once the baby arrives.

There's not much to say, really. I enjoy the solitude.

She looks at my body, trying to take in my largeness.

Are the books still all death and gloom?

Always I say good-humoredly, and ask her about her non-profit job. She is happy to talk about herself for a bit.

My friend has aged since giving birth, the impact is visible on her face, on her hair, shoulders, and smiles. There is a fault or fallacy in her appearance. A twitch is always ready to expose her. The last time I saw her (pre-baby) she joked about things that she believed were funny. Today, her presence is translu-cent and her attention scattered, even though her child is not with her. She is still not really here. But I suppose I should commend her for trying.

———

In between bites of soup and sandwich my friend announces *I hate pumping.* She says that she always feels like she's walking into the office smelling of warm milk and not remembering what she is meant to be doing at her desk. They set up this windowless room for her that's the size of a closet. Not those walk-in closets but the ones where your jacket touches the wall as soon as you hang it up. And she always forgets something for pumping, a random lid, an ice pack, or leaves milk-filled bottles in the communal refrigerator overnight.

But the work itself is fine she says, trying to convince me, seemingly wanting to talk about something else.

So, are you excited? she asks. *I bet John is excited. He'll be such a good father, tending to your every need.*

I nod kindly, thinking she is probably right, but I am stuck wondering about how much she has changed. Or is she more like herself now that she has had a baby?

I'm not sure, I've never been good at friendships.

Whatever did happen, I decide then and there, at that over-rated place, that I'm not going to end up like my friend. I am not going to let motherhood drag me through the mud. I know better.

This ingrained reflex of judgment is impossible to shake off, and I recognize that I'm being harsh on her. It's awkward that I can't quite control it, but here we are.

After our lunch and when we say goodbye she hugs me tighter than I'm used to, as if she is convinced that we won't see each other again for an unidentified length of time. Before we part ways, she passes on some unrequested advice, saying something about how once the baby arrives *the key is to stop wanting things,* and I have no idea what she is talking about.

The lights are on because it is early evening. The glass jar of moss on the windowsill is looking lifeless. We have been sitting in silence for what seems like a long time. Peter and his tank have returned to the small dining table. He places a hand around a mug filled with tea but doesn't drink from it. He says that he can't go on for much longer, and his voice is so cracked he must not have had any water all day, perhaps this is the first time that he is talking. I wish he would drink from his cup.

Button can be found on the carpet in the middle of the room, lying on her back like a bug that has accidentally turned the wrong way. John is still at work but should be making his way home soon. Things are not the same when John is not home.

Peter says *You have liberty.* I am free to speak my mind if I desire. The walls are ready to take it. The tank beside him makes an ever-so-slight and short hiss, maybe indicating its last batch of oxygen. He turns to the window, through which a pair of doves can be found perched on a railing, seemingly waiting. I walk over to the couch and lean on a dome of laundry. I press my face into the pile of clothes and let uneven silences occur between us. By now they are expected, and they don't impose or require too much attention. However short-lived, they comfort and protect. It gives me room to explain once I lift my head back up.

This is your life and you're so deep in it that you can't unmake it, you can't unbirth your baby because she wishes to be alive, you can't remake your career, there's no way you'll be a professional dancer anymore or join the philharmonic, don't even fantasize about one day becoming that avant-garde independent filmmaker because you're here, feeling like you did when your mother died but now wondering who around you thinks it's of importance to know how difficult it is to nurse? Or how often you are covered—down to your elbows—in feces when changing diapers? What difference does it make if anyone knows the quantity of laundry that is created between these four walls? Or the hanging of the laundry, the folding of the laundry. Who wants to recognize the repetition? Who cares about what domesticity is made of?

The very thing that brought us into this world and its conditions are spat upon.

The putting away of clothes, the filling up the box of wipes with new wipes, the unpacking diapers from boxes, the ordering more diaper cream, or tissues, the wiping butt cheeks, the wiping milk-dribble from shoulders, chins, couches, the soaking of soiled clothes in OxiClean, the emptying the diaper pail, the whiff of shit as you put a knot on the heavy plastic bag, the bassinet needs new sheets, flush the Oxi-feces water from the bucket down the toilet, doing your best to avoid getting shit on your fingers, wash your hands, don't get a stomach bug, don't look in the mirror, best to change your blood-soaked pad while the baby is not in your arms, remember first you squirt with water and then you *pat your vagina,* don't let the blood scare you, don't forget to numb the pain with athletes' spray, pull up your mesh undies, pick up the baby, hold it, hold, hold, don't you dare let go.

All this doing and no poetry, I say to Peter.

I describe the utter shame that has enveloped me since we brought Button home from the hospital.

Yet the desire exists Peter injects, wisely and ghostlike, but also maybe something is lost in translation.

The man must be dying if he has this kind of patience for such a hysterical woman, and my debilitating state hinders me from apologizing to my neighbor.

Through his broken English, Peter implies that love comes with sacrifices. The important kind of love does not exist without the existence of certain losses. It remains to be seen which loss is possible enough to bear, to endure, to relinquish.

It's time I go he says, and I don't fully understand the gravity of this simple sentence until it is too late. Peter is a fog that lifts, smoke that evaporates, a tide receding.

The one-man play transitions smoothly and when John comes through the door, he finds me in the same spot, except Button is screaming. He picks her up from the floor and slides her into one side of his arm. They sit down beside me and the pile of clothes. She is still discontent, but a little less so than before.

What's going on? he asks more like a statement than a question.

I can't tell you what I'm thinking.

Why not?

If I do, you'll take her away from me.

What makes you think that?

John gives me a serious face. Button is looking not at us but through us. Thankfully, she can't tell on me.

You need more sleep he says solemnly and perhaps because he is unwilling to hear more.

Button is passed back to me. He walks over to the kitchen because feeding me makes him appear less powerless. I don't say anything and he doesn't say anything else. I hear him open and close the fridge a couple of times. Soon enough, he has engineered a meal for me. Walking over to the couch with a filled plate, he asks

Does he still come by?

Sometimes. I trade him Button for the food, and for a little while he watches me eat.

What if you stopped opening the door? he asks, but I'm barely listening. It doesn't take long until I leave an empty plate on the cushion next to me. Whatever he made was delicious, makes me almost delirious.

I find it disturbing, that's all he says. Again, I can't register his attempt at understanding.

I move like a contraption that's about to go off, and he can tell that the plug needs to be pulled on me.

Look, why don't I wake you when she needs you he suggests, and in whatever clothes I am still in and without having washed my face or brushed my teeth, John lets me go lie down in bed. I am so tired it hurts, and by the time my head hits the pillow I am sleeping.

Pain shoots from my pelvis up my spine and I wake as if the smoke alarm in the apartment has gone off. At first I don't know where I am. The apartment is completely dark, everyone is asleep but me. I can't hear Button breathing. I put my arm out in the dark over her bassinet, hoping to feel my way to her rising and sinking chest. There she is. I wait for the movement. Softly, it comes. Reliable, those waves on a shore.

In the dark bedroom, awake between my child and my husband, I continue to be plagued by unrest. I can hear all the way down to our street: someone throws a glass bottle against the pavement, a cat whines in pain or to express another emotion. There's a drunken brawl, maybe even a mugging, unless my mind is taking too drastic of a turn. Someone enters the double doors to our building. They are either returning home or making a late-night visit.

The fridge kicks into a low hum and distracts me. I turn to John, who looks undeniably handsome or at least innocent, even in his sleep.

I move and Button wakes from the crack of my wrist. A slow whimpering comes from her, she can hear my unease and senses all my moves. I scoot up in bed and lean against the wall. There's the gentle scrunching of the pillow and a slight swoosh of the duvet. I pull my nursing bra to the side and expose a heavy breast to the night. Somehow my nipple appears darker within the darkness of the room.

With my exposed chest, I turn and scoop Button up with a pair of tired arms. I hold her neck with both hands as if I am about to drink from a goblet. As I raise her toward me the milk bar is officially open, and I welcome my only customer.

Even in the dark she finds the milk, and while she is drinking I collect her body into place. I lift an arm, reposition a leg. Her body yields on every occasion. She trusts me with her whole still-unlived life. It's a responsibility that excites and revolts me at the same time. My mouth, for example, is so big compared to

hers. If I wanted to, I could cover her entire mouth with mine
and if I kiss her on the mouth, there is no way for her to not let
me. Should I be kissing her on the mouth?

The utter helplessness of a baby is infuriating. They can't
even consider how exposed their bodies are. What if I widen
the exposure and drop her out of the window? What if I let a
delivery man come and collect her? What if I turn away for a
second and the things I care most deeply about are lost to me
forever? The night protects her and yet, the night is my ruin.

Once Button has slowed down and is done with one side, I
lift her up to my shoulder and gently pat her on the back, waiting for air to emanate from her tiny body. We sit like this until
I decide to move us into the nursery. Together we pass the
mountainous shadows the laundry makes at night and sit down
on a chair. I turn on the noise machine and give her the other
breast. There we continue in darkness. Slowly, the contours of
the room begin to appear. Unshapely reflections distinguish
themselves. The blinds are down, someone's air-conditioning
next door is drumming. My thoughts are muffled by the sound
of the noise machine, it sends me closer to sleep. But if I sleep,
I will drop the baby and I should not drop the baby.

As she drinks from the other tit, the steady white noise infil-
trates my consciousness. To hear myself think, my thoughts
have to yell.

But I want to be free.

The dark room swallows my sentence. Button's eyes are
closed like any newborn pup's. The noise machine doesn't fal-
ter. I continue screaming:

Let me be a child.

If only I could sit at my desk. I turn to the dim walls around
us. My nose starts to run and my belly is squished by the

weight of Button. I wipe my nose with the back of my hand and it's impossible not to feel pitiable. My legs are tight and sore from not moving enough. My neck crackles, my back crumbles forward, and my eyes are dry from the contained air. The size of the apartment is the contour of my body. Traces of tears and dirt and sweat and gunk surface in all our combined corners as crust and goo. I am a prisoner of my own making. After all, I made Button and I wanted her, and now I can't get out.

Why can't you give me a mother?

Button passes out and we are done with both sides. I am envious of the complete release in her body, total truth, total oblivion. Is this the definition of "pure"? My bank of vocabulary is fading farther away from me. I go to put her down in a corner of the couch and turn to the kitchen to forage for an immediate meal.

I hit a hard-boiled egg against the counter and peel the shell into the sink. I scarf it down in three bites without salt. I take chunks from an apple and break off a piece of parmesan cheese, mixing the different tastes in my mouth. I munch on baby carrots until they make me cough. I spoon ricotta straight out of the container and grab a handful of almonds from a cabinet. I see a half-opened box of crackers and fill each cheek full. I wash the sustenance down with water, chugging it back relentlessly.

I thought I

loved her in theory, but

I hated her as Button,

as everything I think of and everything that I am. What am I anymore?

I still wobble when I walk, as if she once kept my body in balance.

Google,

I suppose
I used to believe in
scribbling in notebooks
writing letters
sealing envelopes shut
slipping notes
riding bicycles
letting go of the handlebars
walking barefoot
blowing dandelion seed heads &
eating gelato
or going for a walk
I used to appreciate
magic (the kind that children believe in, the kind that hides
behind ears and
disappears in multiwalled boxes) I believed in
poetry (of course) and
nonsense, also
daffodils
reading until the book falls down on your chest

lying in the shade
staring
napping
clouds
succumbing to the sky
reading poetry by a windowsill
journaling by a windowsill
the windowsill
the tops of trees
sunlight through leaves
the library
the corridor of books
the smell of dust, the tickle in your nose
falling in love, immediately & foolishly
sex
sleeping in
other people
making palm-sized art for other people
talking to strangers, flirting
during concerts
trees
sunsets
holding hands
language.

Is everything all right? Peter asks.

The next morning, when I'm home alone with Button but in the returned company of my neighbor, I find out about the knives. They're not where they are usually kept, and their disappearance is immediately obvious in the kitchen drawer. This includes my one good knife that was added to John's more elaborate collection. But after some random searching I see that John hasn't hidden all sharp objects from me, only the knives. He doesn't seem worried that I'll poke Button's eyes out with one of our forks, but I suppose I shouldn't give him any more ideas.

From the kitchen, I walk over to Peter with a new warm cup of tea. Button is asleep in her container next to him.

My husband has hidden the knives.

He puts one hand on the cup, while the other clutches the tank like there is a chance that it will run away. He asks me if that's normal.

I wouldn't say that it is.

I come around and sit down in front of him.

Do you need one?

Not at this moment, I suppose.

Maybe he is giving you a favor. He sips from the beverage in front of him, masking as someone who is content, being the one with all the answers.

Do you think there's something wrong with me? My question is aimed at Peter even though I'm looking at Button.

No more than other person he says. The light in the room is kind and gives his skin a soft hue. I can see through it.

Do you only live to think of her? I ask carelessly.

Persze he agrees.

He gives a tired exhale and readjusts one of the tubes behind his ear.

She was good companion.

He admits he was never sure what he gave but tried to be a good husband.

I am struck by an uneven dose of jealousy from hearing Peter speak about his wife, and Button wakes herself with a deep breath as if she has been chased in her sleep. She grunts nervously. I pick her up and pull one part of my robe to the side. I unbuckle the top of my bra. I cup my breast and angle it up to Button's open mouth and pair the two with each other. By now, there's nothing tense about exposing myself in front of Peter.

While Button is sucking away at the breast, unaware of the slight turn of events, I return to my conflicted emotions and wish and yearn that John were at home with us.

A sense of conviction arrives, delicately, but it arrives.

We don't have much time I tell John. He is cradling me on the couch. There's a spot on his T-shirt that's wet. At the end of my sentence, John squeezes and lullabies me.

I know, I know.

I apologize for being emotional. Inside our embrace, he swoops in a hand and squeezes one of my breasts. My body jiggles like a waterbed.

They're so big these days.

I know, it's crazy.

I like it.

Me too.

He takes my phone and scrolls through the baby app that shows you which fruit or vegetable the fetus is most comparable to. A technological cliché you have access to during the pregnancy that aims to comfort the soon-enough mother.

How can you go from eggplant to corn on the cob? John asks. That makes no sense. We both know an eggplant is larger than corn on the cob. I giggle in a kind of stupidity or innocence with the waves of hormones pumping through my body, deflecting all the discomfort that comes along with a baby growing inside of you.

Zucchini, cauliflower, acorn squash . . . the whole medley is here.

Stop, you're making me hungry I say and try to grab my phone back from him. We wrestle and giggle and tease and tickle until I lose my breath. I push myself away from his loving arms, still laughing, and turn to the fridge. John returns to his own phone and babbles away, mostly to himself, about all the things that we still need to prepare for the baby's arrival. There is time and also no time at all. His anxiousness is endearing. I'm still mainly thinking about food, since the body does what the body needs. In Swedish, *kropp*—a compressed round mass, a group, a crop of harvest, fruit, plant, or the crop of a bird. Essentially, the body is an enlarged esophagus. Food can be kept here. Milk can be produced. A secretion of cells lines the body and feeds newly hatched chicks.

So much of what I am going through these days is out of my control. There is a mind but the body rules. The heart beats for the baby, the blood flows to the baby, the air travels to the baby. I am the stupid vessel, through and through. Can a childbearing woman be any more of an alien?

I think of cows and deer and horses that lick their little ones dry right after birth. I think of the amniotic sac that cracks when the foal falls to the ground. The cord that kept us alive all these months is cut and we are set free. It's all quite powerful and sublime. We are at our most alive.

A fruit fly tickles my nostrils as it flies by and around. My scalp itches, my cuticles are picked back, my body is unsettled, stitches prickling, mesh wedging into thigh creases. I am unmoored. I move my eyes faster than my head but that doesn't matter, it's already gone.

Things turn unreliable in the dark. Button is also a terrible alibi.

We are sitting still in the nursery but our bodies talk in multitudes of motion. Heavy breathing, slow humming, the odd twitch, the constant itch, don't think too much about it, but I do, because what else is there but thinking. We have been sitting like this for some time since I last changed and fed Button and I think it's time for us to go back to the bedroom, but I'm scared to unsettle her. I am also too tired to hold on for much longer. I need to lie down. I need relief. *Relieve, relever, relevare.* Raise me from my burden. Almost like *lättnad* in Swedish, but I like *befrielse* more because it implies "freedom." I am trying to convince myself of something that I don't believe in.

Fatigue kicks in and all my rational thinking leaves me.

I walk us back to the bedroom, I am enveloped in exhaustion. I lay Button down in the bassinet next to the bed, and it's like she can smell the distance between us. She begins to cry for fear of abandonment. I have to pick her up again, otherwise she will grow in noise and wake John, and John needs his sleep.

She quiets when I pick her back up and it's obvious that I have already lost this game. So I give in and walk us away from the bedroom again and sit us down on the couch and I give in and I lean back and I give in and I fall asleep and with her in my arms I give in and the sleep is immediate.

Instant satisfaction washes over me, although I am already unconscious before I can enjoy it.

When I wake later in the day, I hear shuffling and feel the harsh light from outside. It's like I woke up into a headache. John is awake, too, and with us in the apartment. The shuffling, the light, and John's presence indicate that it's the weekend, which means we have made it through our first week together as mother and baby. The walls of the building across from ours sizzle. I can't hear the air but I can think it. John comes over to us in the bedroom and tells me I need to go outside. He carries a serious face.

Please take the baby out for a walk, get some air he says. He starts stroking Button's head. She stares through him and waves her tentacle arms, legs.

Or leave her here for a bit. If you're worried about going too far, walk around the building.

He even says that I can go and get an overpriced coffee. The man is serious.

I can smell the burning coal from the side-stoop barbecues and imagine that there are people gathered around, sitting on camp chairs and drinking lukewarm beer or leaning on fences, smoking blunts, kicking dirt, chasing their kids around, walking their dogs, sipping burned deli coffee, riding bikes, scooters, what have you. The activities of a neighborhood are pumping outside our small two-bedroom apartment; I am not an idiot. And yet, I am a Miffo.

Later I say.

I sound like an addict trying to be honest but failing. He goes on to say that we have to start figuring things out, the pediatrician messaged asking us to come back, some shot was missing from Button's medical records and John can't keep leaving the office during the week.

Okay, maybe later I say.

John looks at me without saying anything else and lets me lie, lets me stand by my desolation, walks away and leaves me alone. He goes about his ways, about his life, his interests, sorts his papers, polishes his shoes, exercises, makes a smoothie for himself, empties the recycling, runs an errand, and lets me sit and soak in my lie, in the shameful envelopment of denial.

I live in the crease between two words.

It's a harsh summer's day in the city, I'm a small number of weeks away from giving birth and attempting to get as much translating done as possible before the baby arrives. To kill two needs with one walk, I have wobbled over to a pastry shop down the street from our apartment. I'm sitting by the window, and the movements outside are constant but not exhausting. There's a sweet *lagom* pace to the afternoon, that in-between time of things: not quite dinner, but we have certainly moved on from lunch.

I'm drinking chamomile tea and waiting for a slice of napoleon cake to be brought to me. The tea is for the baby and the pastry is for me. I'm also writing, and revel in the pages that I have to get through to keep my schedule. I am in the middle of a good part of the novel; I've already read the entire book at least once, so I know what leads to the man's suicide and how the wife will move on, but now my biggest motivation is to get the *message* of each sentence across. Be the writer, interpret the part. I want to move the pace from the page I'm reading to the page that I'm writing. At the same time as I'm translating, I'm making a list of questions that I want to ask the author and a list of notes for the editor who will eventually polish up my English. This is the kind of leisurely afternoon work that I appreciate the most—the flow before the many pauses.

In the lively pastry shop, I would be fine with admitting that I have never been a woman with many needs. There is no mark I need to make. What I appreciate about translations is spending time in the no-man's-land between words from two different languages that may or may not mean similar or even the same thing. In this land, I find that the point is not to reach "sameness"—the mirror of the translation is still a reflection, but it should be about representation. The distinctions are not blurred because you see both words clearly. Culture (and therefore also history) prevails over the capability of each language. And, ultimately, there must be respect. Of course, there are exceptions, and it is in those exceptions that the translator has choices. The translator always makes choices, even if the reader ends up viewing it to be the wrong or flawed one.

A kick from the belly makes me wonder about the choices of a mother. Does a mother have language? Can she grow her own mother tongue? Or only pass it on ... What about agency? How does it manifest?

My napoleon arrives with a single jiggle when the waitress sets it down on the table. Before I can ask for a fork, she is already on to the next thing.

I'll be right back I whisper to the cake and get up to grab one. The café is busy with informal job interviews, students plugged in to their laptops, and couples encouraging their in-laws to indulge in a sweet treat. People give me space once they see the bump—I must look like something that will go off if you stand too close. Watch out, folks, I'll detonate!

Back to the napoleon and back to the questions. I can't scoot my chair very close to the table, but it's all right.

While I'm cutting bite-sized pieces with a fork and getting cream all over my plate, I take notes. My movements with the pen are nonchalant, the sugar from the cake is already having an impact on my mood. I put a hand on my belly like it's always been there and feel pleased with myself.

I am only this moment.

He took her again without me.

John explains what happened and how the events unfolded. For him, it was a straightforward hour spent with Button, but I can barely take it. I want to rip my hair out, toss my head back like I'm in hysterics, climb the walls, jab my thighs.

Button cried her first tear at the pediatrician. The vaccine shot in her tiny thigh reverberated through her small body and the very first tear of her life rolled out of her eye and slid down her cheek, all the way down into the small seashell of an ear. Her face shook with red. Her mouth widened as harshly as the scream she let out. It made the back of her tongue shake. Even though I was absent, I can see it in front of me.

It was the smallest, simplest drop John says. And yet it was noticeably a tear.

You fail immediately as a mother. As a mother, you have immediately failed. And, for the rest of the day, I don't get out of bed.

The apartment quickly turns on itself. Dirty diapers accumulate a funky, creamy, and plastic smell, and dishes pile in the sink. In her first feverish state, Button cries relentlessly. Her wails echo through the apartment. John tries his hand at soothing her, he shushes and squeezes, comforts and cuddles. She seems to eventually release into sleep, I can't hear her anymore. John comes into the bedroom empty-handed, looking exhausted. He sits down next to me. Says it is time for me to come outside.

This is not fun anymore.

He puts a hand on my shoulder.

I hide under the covers, ignore the pressure from my chest, deny my responsibilities, fold into fatigue, and try to avoid John's eyes.

How long are you going to keep doing this?

The weight of his hand is both heavy and light.

It's been days and you've not left the apartment. To this reasoning he adds: *You can't keep on doing this—you are not yourself.* Another squeeze on the shoulder. I lift the cover off my head.

What was I before? This is not what he expects to hear, and John starts to cry.

This is a rarity. John cries like some men do. It is subtle, barely visible, but his eyes do tear up. He tries to push the tears back in, and his eyes become damp underneath.

There is only slight pleasure and instead a great deal more pain to witness John this upset. Well?

John?

Not this he says.

Not this.

He apologizes but he has to go back to work, he has already been gone from the office for too long, which means that another way of saying "He took her again without me" is "I made him go without me."

There's dripping from above.

When I trace the crack from our bed, I see it branching off into textures of dark blues, greens, and grays. I've not seen these colors before on the ceiling. I consider waking John to ask him if the cracks appear longer to him, but won't he just say they've always been there?

It's the first part of the evening and so far so good with Button in her bassinet. We haven't hit midnight yet, the night hasn't fully unleashed.

A drop of water falls onto the side of my forehead. I look up and a slight shine from a few heavy drips confirms that we are lying right under a thick dome of moisture. Should I do something? John will brush my imagination away. Another drop insists—I should do something.

I quietly step out of bed and, in the dark, I reach for my robe. There is still time to reconsider this while I tie the belt around my waist. Instead I slip on a pair of shoes in the hallway and leave the door partly open so I don't have to take any keys.

In the stairway, a harsh yellow light blinks on automatically. My eyes need an extra second to adjust and as I shuffle up the stairs, disturbing images appear in front of me. They are either my demise or my liberation. While I'm in the stairway, Peter's floor caves in. The debris covers Button completely. That's the end of her. The crash happens so forcefully that it's impossible to know for sure if Button died from suffocation or from being crushed. John manages to stay unharmed because he is John and he hasn't done anything wrong. I am to blame because I am the mother who left her infant. John divorces me after the trauma of having lost our only child. Eventually, I scramble together a new life in some other city, living an even more modest life than before, cooped up in a one-bedroom apartment that under no circumstances can face a playground for fear of seeing any children through the window. Translation is all I'm left with. I am no longer a mother. I never leave the apartment.

The imagined scenario concludes when I reach Peter's door. There wasn't even vertigo, and yet I don't know how I made it out. The realization is my liberation, of sorts. The days inside the apartment have come to an end, and I pull the belt of the robe tighter around my waist. This time, I am doing the knocking. I hear shuffling and then there's silence. The door opens and Peter peeks his head out. I see mostly a wide forehead and a pair of tired old eyes squinting from the light.

What do you want? he asks, and I don't fully know where to begin but I know that I don't have much time.

There's a leak. Water is dripping.

No leak he says. I must be making this up. He says I should go back to sleep. Peter is closing the door on me.

Good night he adds.

Wait.

We are quiet for a beat and from the stillness in the stairway, a distinguished and painful exclamation emerges below.

Peter says that my baby is crying, and I am running out of time.

Sorry I say. *I just think there's something wrong with our ceiling.*

I beg him to let me in for a second and then promise that I will leave him alone as soon as I've taken a look.

Peter's eyes still contain life but the hunch is worrisome, his body is trying to say something. The old man lowers his head slightly, he is about to close the door, he closes the door, but he also moves the tank. Together they take a few steps back so that they can let me in.

I walk slowly past Peter and the tank, fully aware that both of our lives are going to change after this visit. The air is incredibly moist like I'm in a terrarium. From the darkly lit room I need to center myself. My eyes need to adapt. There's something larger than me taking up most of the space. At first, I don't know what it is that is in front of me; some oddly large or ill-placed sculpture demanding attention in the middle of the room.

Later, when I will explain it to John, I will tell him that it was a gigantic boulder. It was held up by a wooden construct and the stone sat in a low pool of murky water. John will listen and believe me because he loves me. The earthy smell of the room brings me back to where Peter and I are. We can't be in the city anymore and yet, we still are. The boulder is lit by a series of low dangling lights that are hooked up to a timer, which is discreetly ticking away in a corner. A long hose snakes around and over the stone. It is held up by a delicate construct, a kind of arm in a cast midair. Water runs carefully out of the hose in a slow-flowing stream, dripping meditatively onto the stone. The stone shimmers before us, showing off an unsentimental beauty, and it's difficult to look elsewhere. Something begins to purr at my feet, trying to flirt with me. Agata's black cat circles in eights around my ankles, also asking to be noticed.

Only after I've taken in the different contrasts of light in the room do I see what it is that I have so easily overlooked. The sight of it glows so obviously in front of me that I'm embarrassed to have missed it. The color is emerald-like in power.

She was better at this.

Peter says that Agata couldn't help herself; she built a carpet of moss, and since her death he has tried to maintain the construct but it's impossible, *lehetetlen.*

The man garbles his words, he acts tired and hungry or like he is about to cry and doesn't know where to put his arms, they are so long. The unbearableness of the situation is here. Time must also be running out for Peter.

Following the water from the stone, I can see that it goes beyond the murky pond. It is soaked into the wooden construct and into a carpet that centers the room. I was, in a way, right. We may fall through the floor any minute.

If I don't do something the boulder will collapse through the soggy ceiling and ruin our home. The walls won't hold anymore, my marriage will be over, my child will have lost her mother.

Miffo needs to leave.

Oh, Peter.

We may still be all right today, but not tomorrow.

I don't think I can do this anymore.

If I don't do something it will all cave in.

No.

If I don't leave this building, Peter may take me down with him.

We can't do this anymore.

I have to leave.

And you must go.

Congratulations, Mama! an excited stranger yells from the other side of the street as I'm sitting on our stoop, eating ice cream. The sun beams.

Thank you!

I raise my sticky hand. It's one of those four-dollar ice creams, but the guy at the deli enjoys displaying his fondness toward my big belly and only wants three dollars.

The chocolate melts faster than I can lick it. The cream runs down my fingers and palm, and I extend my greed by licking my hand. The stoop is not the most comfortable place in the world, but my legs are tired and my lower back aches, there's so much front weight to carry now. I've ballooned to my limit and often need to stop to catch my breath.

And there is always room for ice cream.

I run a finger along the big dome of belly and the sugar ignites little kicks, making the skin protrude in uneven bulges.

What are you in there? Lilla säl.

Little seal, what are you.

Drops of chocolate land on my stretchy dress before I get to catch it. It's tricky to get the smudge out and I make it worse rather than better but it's okay, I don't care how gluttonous I may seem. I'm a round pile of liberation right now. Full of life. Watch me.

I ask John to sit down on the couch with me, the sweet and boring epicenter of our home. He joins me and rests his neck on the cushion, which makes him stare up at the ceiling. The rupture above us looms large and wide, showing shadowy contours. A large threatening cloud of mold hangs over us. It is time.

At some point, when this is all over, I will look up where the word "submission" comes from. The word will acquire new meaning as I will begin to use it. But first, let me try and say:

We used to get excited at the sight of each other.

What do you mean? he asks.

You would do this thing. You looked up when I showed up. Whatever it was that you were doing, wherever we were, you always stopped and took me in.

I still do that.

Not since she arrived.

John pauses.

It's only been a few weeks and we're both exhausted.

I just miss that tremendously. And now I feel like I'm in this all alone.

That's not true.

He squeezes me out of reflex.

Well, that's what it feels like. Okay—Can't you let me explain?

Okay, fine.

And I keep having these terrible thoughts of hurting her.

You're not going to hurt her.

How can you be so sure? I am not going to mention the knives.

John pauses on that note, not mentioning the knives.

Let me try to get some time off he finally suggests, and gives me another squeeze. *I'll wrangle some free days together. And let's get you more sleep, more help.*

John was trying to be there all along.

The exhaustion in my body releases, the body itself gives in and cries. John lets me tremble for a bit, waits for me to finish, waits. The light in the apartment is gentle, even though the ceiling might drop down on us at any minute.

Let's go get some air. I think we all need it and before I get the chance to object John plucks Button up from her slumber and makes his way to the door. She hangs limp but not lifeless in his arms. A little more confident this time around, he straps her onto his chest. Readies my shoes in the hallway.

First he whispers her name as if he is still trying it out and then he tells me mine so I don't confuse it with someone like Miffo. From his mouth we sound like the taste of fresh fruit. It is difficult to resist John.

I put my shoes on but leave my face unwashed. With Button strapped to John's chest I follow my family outside and the relief of having a pair of free hands stills the mind. We walk past the notice board and see that there's a new piece of paper pinned to the wall. The note announces a memorial service seven blocks away, four days from today. It includes a picture of Peter when he must have been ten or fifteen years younger. In the picture, he is still handsome and free of his tank.

Does it say how he died? John wonders and holds the door open for me. I shake my head and touch the photocopied image of our neighbor. The man has a twinkle in his eye, someone dear to him took this picture.

It doesn't say much, just the time and place of the service.

We agree to try to attend.

Past the double doors and newly arrived at our stoop, I wish to sit down.

Can I sit for a minute? Only for a second or two, but I would very much like to sit down. It's been a while since I looked up at the sky.

Sure, of course John says. He continues down the steps and stops by the pavement, a few feet below me. He peeks down on his chest to check in on Button, then takes in our street with deep inhales and wide panoramic eyes. It's another late afternoon in the city. The bright and burning star is getting ready to hide behind our building.

Button gives John a tilted smirk, completely unaware that it makes her resemble a drowsy miniature old man. She signals contentment by making minor sounds, mostly out of curiosity about what is around her, what lights are shining on her face or where a slight breeze touches her skin. From where I sit I see that the two of them make a good pair.

The golden hour reflects off our skin and I am reminded: it is my favorite time of the day.

ACKNOWLEDGMENTS

Kate Johnson saw something in my writing long before Miffo started scratching at my door. She is my agent, friend, fellow artist, mama confidante, and I am indebted to her. I will forever feel that I can't thank you enough.

Thank you to everyone at Wolf Literary Services for being so kind to me, especially Kirsten Wolf.

Thank you, Lisa Lucas, for encouraging me to "tell the whole last truth." Your unwavering belief in this book made me finally believe in myself as a writer, and I'm in awe of your force.

Throughout the editing process, Juliet Mabey added incredibly thoughtful and generous notes. Thank you for the care you have put into these pages, and for helping me get the leaky tits right.

There are so many people involved in producing and publishing a book, and I appreciate everyone at Pantheon Books and Oneworld Publications for championing this one. For the many little things that were handled with ease, passion, and kindness, thank you to Zachary Phillips, Sarah Pannenberg, Amara Balan, Polly Hatfield, Kate Bland, Lucy Cooper, and Hayley Warnham. For patiently handling my intentional foreignness and unintentional typos, thank you to Nicole Pedersen and Karen Thompson. A special thank-you to Michiko Clark, whose enthusiasm is infectious. Thank you to Camilla Ferrier, Jemma McDonagh, and Brittany Poulin at the Marsh Agency for all your hard work. Also, Saliann St-Clair—you're amazing.

Thank you to Linda Huang for designing such a stunning first jacket, and to Ben Mistak for making me look good.

Agata's work and the passages on moss were inspired by Robin Wall Kimmerer's *Gathering Moss* and Jerry Jenkins's Northern Forest Atlas project. I appreciate Maximilian Blaustein's help with checking that, for this piece of fiction, it more or less made sense.

I'm grateful to the first international editors who saw something in Miffo: Flavio Moura and Ana Paula Hisayama, Olivier Espaze, Ádám Halmos and Ákos Déri. A special thank-you to Friederike Schilbach for saying *Yes, absolutely, keep going* when I only had a few pages to show. If you only knew how much that meant to me at the time.

Speaking of early drafts, thank you to Kyle Kabel, Melanie LaBarge, and Jana-Maria Hartmann for such insightful feedback and continuous support. A part of me feels like once I started telling friends what I was working on, I was writing for all of them. Like Erin Edmison and Beniamino Ambrosi; thank you both for your beautiful friendship, but also for believing in me as a writer. Those two things don't always come hand in hand.

When I first arrived in Austin, I was welcomed into a writing group, which also kept me going—thank you Adeena Reitberger, Amanda Faraone, Marta Evans, Katie Angermeier Haab, and Tayler Heuston for cheering me on even with the first messy pages.

For the many talks about art, literature, and writing over the years—thank you Ursel Allenstein, Hans Jürgen Balmes, Deni Ellis Béchard, Peter Blackstock, Peter Harper, Mary Krienke,

Laura Mamelok, Julie Paludan-Müller, Mikkel Rosengaard, Amy Marie Spangler, and Cathrin Wirtz.

If people can have "partners in crime" can I have a sister-in-writing? Olga Vilkotskaya, you would know what I mean. I am very lucky to have you in my life.

Thank you to my families—the Molnars, the Grosskopfs, the Martins—for their unbound generosity, love, and support.

Thank you to Vera for making me a better writer, and to Emery for making me a happier one.

I started writing this novel sometime in 2018, and I wouldn't have made it through these past years without the love from my husband. This book is dedicated to him.

A NOTE ABOUT THE AUTHOR

Szilvia Molnar is the foreign rights director at a New York–based literary agency and the author of a chapbook, *Soft Split*. Her work has appeared in *Guernica, Lit Hub, Triangle House Review, Two Serious Ladies, The Buenos Aires Review,* and *Neue Rundschau*. Born in Budapest, Molnar was raised in Sweden. She lives in Austin, Texas.

A NOTE ON THE TYPE

This book was set in Janson, a typeface named for the Dutchman Anton Janson, but is actually the work of Nicholas Kis (1650–1702). The type is an excellent example of the influential and sturdy Dutch types that prevailed in England up to the time William Caslon (1692–1766) developed his own incomparable designs from them.

Composed by North Market Street Graphics
Lancaster, Pennsylvania

Printed and bound by Berryville Graphics
Berryville, Virginia

Designed by Michael Collica